KAMINSKIELOY @GMAIL.COM

8083730793

NATASHA

NATASHA

ELOY KAMINSKI

Hawaii, USA

NATASHA
ELOY KAMINSKI
English version

First Edition: 2023
ISBN

Cover Artwork by Eloy Kaminski

Cover design: Alejandra Garcia

Layout for print and digital Book: Julio C. Zani
www.publicatulibro.com

Translation: All the stories were translated by Eric Winter except:
"The Golem", "The Book is Real" and "The Final Tale" which
were translated by Ian Barnett, and "The Lost Child," which was
translated by Ian Barnett and edited by Eric Winter.

"For Norma,
for her incredible evolution
and development".

THE PRICE OF YOUR ACTIONS

I SAW him and I fell in love. I immediately knew we were destined for each other, that our love would be eternal. Our conversations stretched till dawn, our souls becoming entwined. Violent, mad, demented passion overwhelmed us. I knew we would build a happy life, forge a road together, a path toward the happiness of life. So when he decided to leave me, I was crushed. How much torture, how much anguish can the soul of a woman contain? How could he grow tired of me, when ours was a perfect union? Not only did our bodies speak an unmistakable language of their own, one that only we understood, but everything else was equally perfect. Our eyes had a light that emanated from the same source. How many things in common can two people have? Can a soul divide to inhabit two bodies? Two bodies that search for each other, seeking until they merge once more.

But he decided to go away and leave me, and I decided I wouldn't let that be, that he would never leave, that he would stay with me, no matter the cost.

So when I found that book in the library, I wasn't surprised; the book was waiting for me, as though fate had left it there for me, so that I would find it and read it. I knew it was fate; that wondrous force of the universe, that magical hand that brings to a good soul the things it needs. When I found the page with the spell, I knew that it offered the answer I was looking for, the enchantment I could use to keep Eduardo by my side. I read it, devoured it impatiently. A page had been torn out, but that wouldn't interfere with the progress of my plan, because the resolution in the very depths of my being had grown strong, and all the ingredients for the potion and the procedure were intact on the following pages, so I could proceed.

The first step was to buy a fishbowl, the aerator, and some toys for Eduardo to play with and entertain himself. I then set about acquiring the ingredients for the potion, which proved to be a more arduous task than I expected. Nevertheless, I succeeded. I got every last one of them, and then I was ready for the next steps, which weren't terribly difficult. I needed to combine the ingredients to prepare a brew that I would present to Eduardo as a delicious beverage that I had made for him, and I would give it to him during a dinner at which, supposedly, we would talk a little about our situation.

That night arrived. I heard the knock at the door. My heart beat violently with excitement. I ran to open the door.

"Hey, love. How are you? I missed you so much."

"Why did you call me, Magy? I already told you I can't deal with you anymore.

"Don't talk like that, baby. I just want for us to talk a little."

"Everything that had to be said it's been said. What else is there for us to talk about?"

"About us, babe. There's a way for us to stay together."

"Staying together is exactly what I don't want to do. What's more, I have to go. I don't have much time. I'm meeting a friend, and I don't want to keep her waiting."

I noticed that Eduardo's eyes fell upon the fishbowl I had bought. He turned his head toward me and smiled.

"Don't go, baby. Look, I made you something to drink. I put ginger in it, just how you like it. I made dinner too."

"Dinner? But you're a terrible cook. What makes you think I would put anything in my mouth that you've cooked?"

"All right, then. You don't have to get like that. At least have the drink I made you."

"Fine. I'll have the drink, but then I'm leaving."

I ran to the fridge and took out the brew, which was ready and awaiting its moment. I went back to the living room.

"Here it is, love. I hope you like it."

I saw him take the glass, bring it to his nose and smell the contents. My heart pounded in my chest. I saw his hand bring the glass to his lips, where he stopped for a moment. My eyelids opened wide, my heart beat furiously, and my mind glistened with the delicious certainty that in just a moment, Eduardo would be mine forever.

Then Eduardo looked straight into my eyes, smiled one more time, and drank the potion down to the last drop.

He stood before me without saying a word, still smiling. I waited, my soul longing. I watched him impatiently. Then it happened. It took me completely by surprise. I didn't know what to expect. Eduardo shrunk, falling to the ground. In only a moment, he disappeared completely, as though he had never existed. Only his clothing remained on the floor. Joy ran through me like a lightning bolt. I knew I had succeeded, and that Eduardo would now be mine forever. I noticed an almost imperceptible movement on the floor among his scattered clothing. The potion had worked. The metamorphosis was complete.

I picked his shirt up off the floor, and I saw him, tiny and flailing on the rug, desperately opening his gills to find the vital air he needed to keep living. I carefully picked him up, brought him up to my face, and with a triumphant smile I looked into his eyes and put him in the fishbowl.

***

Very well, then. That woman really believed she could trick me, that she was cleverer than me. I immediately guessed her intentions. I knew what she meant to do. So I formed a plan that would allow me to get rid of her once and for all, and all the while she was thinking she could get rid of me.

I never meant her any harm. None at all. I just wanted to stop listening to her inane conversation. My God, the things that woman would say. If she had only understood that we had nothing in common, that we were together because our bodies wanted it so. But that didn't last long. There was no passion, there was nothing. Merely a meeting of hormones and nothing more. Her legs and breasts were all I wanted. Was it so hard to understand? I never loved her, nor could I have. We were too different.

But she didn't get it. The poor woman didn't get anything. Well, now it's too late, too late to understand. The only thing she had to do was let me go, and that was it. I would carry on with my life, and she with hers. But no. She wouldn't have accepted it. I figured it out, I saw it in her eyes, and thus I knew what she intended. I beat her to it. I made a move before she did.

She liked to read. What a shame that she never learned anything from books. But she liked to read, and I knew where to leave the book so that she would find it. And find it she did. How did it not seem suspicious to her that there was a bookmark precisely where the recipe for the potion was? But anyway, that woman didn't realize a thing. She read the recipe but didn't read the warning. She couldn't read it because I tore that page out. The warning clearly stated: "he who lives by the sword dies by the sword," and it explained that one could not do harm to another without that harm being revisited upon them tenfold, that the effect of the potion on the person for whom it was prepared was only momentary, but that the person who intended to do harm would suffer for their action permanently. That's right. Permanently, forever.

"So you wanted us to be together. Well then let it be so. We'll be together forever."

* * *

Eduardo stood before Magy for a moment with a grotesque smile. Magy was no longer Magy. Now she was a fish that leapt and flipped around on the carpet. Eduardo didn't move. He stood where he was, watching the life leave her, watching her die.

The fish that had been Magy finally stopped moving and expired. Then Eduardo drew near to it and picked it up, taking it by the tail, and brought it to the kitchen. The pan was already hot. He took a cutting board, put the fish on it, and used a knife to remove the scales. He opened up the belly and removed the guts. Into the pan he put equal parts butter and extra virgin olive oil, extra virgin for everything. Then he carefully placed the fish in the pan and enjoyed the crackling music of the flesh in contact with the hot oil. When the fish was golden brown on both sides, he put it on the plate, poured himself a glass of wine, and sat down to eat.

After a while, there was nothing more on the plate than the bones. Then Eduardo felt satisfied. He picked up the glass of wine, filled it once more, and he sat down in an armchair in the living room. But as soon as he sat back, the glass slipped from his hand and fell to the floor. Eduardo knew immediately that something bad was happening. He looked confusedly at his hand, which was changing, transforming. It was no longer his hand, but a fin. He looked toward the fishbowl in longing desperation. He needed to reach it soon. There was little time. He made an anguished leap toward the fishbowl as a thought passed through his mind: "He who lives by the sword dies by the sword," perhaps his last thought, and he fell onto the rug, flapping, and desperately opening his gills in search of oxygen.

Honolulu, Hawaii

THE CAT

I SAW him for the first time on the street. It was late, and the moon lit up the sidewalk. From among some cardboard boxes, his silhouette appeared, and I heard him meowing. I stopped. His feline crying was like music, a melodious nocturne that came to me, asking for help, food or caresses. I don't know, but something in his voice was calling me, so I approached.

I never cared for animals, I never loved them, but there was something about this one that drew me irresistibly to him, like a magnet pulls at metal, so I bent down and held out my hand. The little cat came at once and walked between my legs, rubbing himself against me, leaving his scent on my pants and socks. I touched him and he meowed again, this time, a long, high-pitched meow, a musical tone that filled the emptiness of the night. When I put my hand on his head, he looked at me and started purring, arched his back, and rubbed up against my legs again.

So we were already friends. It seemed he accepted me immediately. I wondered what he must have seen in me. Why me? Out of the crowd of passersby who parade down this street and wear away the soles of their shoes on these sidewalks. Why did he choose me?

So we started seeing each other often. I changed the route I took on the way back from work to pass by the street where the cat was. I brought him food and stayed to pet him for a while. Our relationship strengthened over time. The kitty knew what time I passed by his sidewalk and was there waiting impatiently for me. When he saw me turning the corner, there was an expression on his face, a sort of twinkle in his eyes, and I realized that the curl of his lips was a smile, that he had become attached to me and enjoyed my company.

But I never loved him, nor did I like him that much. He was a dirty, flea-ridden cat; he had a droopy ear and walked unevenly, as if one of his paws was defective. I never thought of taking him home—feeding him on the sidewalk was enough. I would have never brought that malodorous cat home.

Then I thought about the money I spent every week feeding him, all the more so because the price of cat food had gone up, and I also thought about the time I wasted going out of my way to that back street, when I could be at home watching TV. So one fine afternoon I decided that enough was enough: it was time to end all this.

***

I saw him for the first time on the street. It was late, and the moon had completely filled the sky, flooding the sidewalk with its light. First I heard his footsteps, and then I saw his shadow appear. An unexpected excitement ran through my body; I instinctively knew that he was the one, that I should get out from between the boxes and approach him. I did so, then meowed and took a few steps. He stopped and looked at me. It seemed to me that he hesitated, but I knew that he was the one, so I had to do something to capture his attention.

I rubbed myself in between his legs and meowed again. I looked at him with tender eyes, tried to seduce him, and when he bent down to caress me, I arched my back and smiled.

There was no doubt that we were friends already. Yes, feline friendship is immediate. So we built a relationship in which he came at the same time every day to feed me. I waited for him enthusiastically and smiled at him every time with the best twinkle in my eyes. I would approach him as soon as I heard his steps, because I knew the sound of his footfall, which had become music to my ears, an anticipation of things to come. However, I knew that I was getting closer, little by little, to the premeditated conclusion of our friendship.

Because I never loved that man. I don't like humans, but I tolerate them because they feed me. One might think that I use them, that my actions are maneuvers to deceive them and convince them that I've developed some affection for them so that they give me food. Then I rub myself against their legs, meow at them sweetly, smile at them amorously—yet it's all a farce. When my stomach is full, it's all over. However, with this guy it was different. I felt for him almost the same indifference that I feel for others, but there was something, there was something else.

***

So things came to a head. The situation was already intolerable, so I decided that something had to be done, that the world wasn't big enough for the both of us, and that this damned creature had to disappear.

It would be easy, a quick maneuver, a withering blow, and thus he would meet his end.

So the next time we met I acted friendly, as always. Nothing would betray my intentions; I was smiling and very happy to see him again.

The time had come. He came up to me. This was my chance.

It all happened in a single instant. He never knew what hit him. Like a lightning bolt, death came to him, and now he's gone; he is no more. Well, his body still exists; it's lying on the sidewalk next to me. I hope the street sweeper will take it away in the morning, but his soul is no longer in this world. I sincerely hope that he is becoming lost in some infernal labyrinth.

Now the moon, like on so many other nights, casts its light onto the sidewalk while I wonder who will be the next one to come feed me, and when I look up at the sky, I see the dirty eyes, the clumsy mustache; in the perfect roundness of the moon I see the hateful face of that man.

Manoa, Hawaii

NATASHA

I KNEW I could find Elvio at Dr. Mariano's house. They get together every Saturday at this time to discuss the direction of their practice and general affairs. I was sure I would find him at the office, and then he would tell me where to find Natasha, who has become incredibly illusive of late, and it seems entirely impossible for me to locate her. No answer on her phone. I've already lost count of my innumerable attempts to talk to her. She's never in her apartment, and I'm afraid I'm going to break her door if I keep knocking on it. She never comes out. She's not there, or she's hiding. I don't know.

I'm going crazy with all of this—everything that I don't know. But what I'm certain of is that the rumors can't be true. She couldn't have done such a thing.

So I have to talk to her, but in order to do that, I need to find her, and none of her friends know where she is, or they don't want to tell me. That leaves only Elvio. He's always been loyal and honest. If he knows where to find her, he'll tell me.

I'm almost at Mariano's house, and from the corner, I'm dismayed to see that the windows of the office are closed. That can only mean that they're not there. Maybe they met elsewhere, or perhaps they broke their habit of meeting on Saturdays. Oh my God! Not today! I can't keep waiting. The doubt is burning inside of me like a hot ember. I need for Natasha to tell me it isn't true, that she didn't do it. I know she would never commit such an act;

she would never sully herself like that. Something so foul, so unspeakable.

I arrived at the door of the house and knocked several times. Then I rang the bell repeatedly. When Mariano opened the door it seemed to me a miraculous relief. Winning the lottery couldn't have brought me such joy.

"Is Elvio here?" I asked him without saying hello.

"Yes, come in. We're having tea."

That was a lie. They would be drinking brandy. Those two drunks were always drinking brandy.

Mariano brought me down the hall to the library. For some reason, they had decided to have their meeting there instead of in the office as usual, which made sense to me. I never understood why they met up in the office.

When I saw Elvio, I breathed a sigh of relief. He was sitting on a comfortable sofa and taking sips from a teacup.

"How's it going, Elvio? I need to speak to you right away."

I was sure the cup had anything but tea in it.

"Eloy, what a surprise," he said to me with a sincere smile.

"Come sit down. I'm telling Mariano a truly remarkable story that I heard from a patient."

Elvio is a psychologist and hears all kinds of stories. I hadn't the slightest interest in listening to any of that, nor did I have the patience. What's more, the doubts were eating at me like an acid, and the only thing I could think about was finding Natasha. Having her close. Hearing from her own lips that this was all pure nonsense, a strange illusion, because it was too twisted and foul to be true.

"No, Elvio. I just need you to tell me where to find Natasha."

"Oh! She bought herself a new car.

"Yeah, I heard that. But I'm not interested in her car. I just want to find her. Do you know where she is?"

"She's probably driving. Since she got that car, that's all she does. It's a beautiful Peugeot 504. That bright blue is a bit much, but it's a smooth ride."

"That's great about the car, but I want to know where she is."

"Hey, listen to this. I'm in the middle of telling Mariano this incredible story. I want you to hear it and see what you think.

So Elvio went back to the story of his patient, and it seemed too imprudent to interrupt him. After all, I was the one who was in a hurry. It didn't seem right to burst into the middle of their get-together and impose my needs, so I mustered the patience I could, made myself comfortable on the couch, and I got ready to listen.

The story he told went more or less like this:

"The patient told me that he believed, beyond a shadow of a doubt, that doppelgängers were not a thing of literary myth, but of the real world. He told me he didn't need to believe the many stories that appear in literature or in people's conversations, because he had his own story.

He told me that at the age of twenty-three, he had struck up a friendship with a rather unusual character. His name was Yabricio and, due to certain family circumstances, he had bloomed early and had developed some peculiarities of character. When he was twenty-one years old, he had left for Brazil to open a restaurant with a certain local character as his partner.

Yabricio also had some physical peculiarities. His back had the definition of a bodybuilder's, though he had never engaged in the endeavor. What's more, he had a very characteristic gesture, a movement that he made with his arm in combination with a facial expression in a way that was highly distinctive, and somehow, a personal trademark.

This young man Yabricio ended up having such an influence on my patient that, for a long time now, he has longed to become a traveler and thus to come in contact with the things of the world. Driven by the example of Yabricio, and in some way inspired by him, my patient decided to pursue his own destiny as a traveler and surrender where the open road might take him.

And so it was that he reached a town called David, and then he went on to Bocas del Toro, a remote location of the Caribbean. It was there, in that hidden place, that he happened upon an individual who seemed a nearly identical replica of his old friend Yabricio.

This new figure was of Italian origin, his name was Paolo, and he was at least ten years older than Yabricio. However the similarities between them were striking, and not limited to the physical. There was a certain unequivocal energy that was identical in the two men. Not only were they incredibly similar in their hair and faces, but so too were they in stature and build. My patient observed that uniquely shaped back of Yabricio's in Paolo as well, and their way of speaking and moving was identical. When my patient surprised Paolo by making that gesture so very characteristic of Yabricio, his distinctive personal trademark, not only was he taken aback in amazement or surprise, but he also realized, all this he told me, that he had come face-to-face with a peculiarity of the universe, a bizarre case of the duplication of a man. He had found in Paolo a double of Yabricio.

My patient told me in addition, that the similarities did not end there. There were also parallels between the personal stories of the two men. He heard Paolo relate that due to family reasons, he had begun a life of business at the age of twenty-one, when he moved to a different region of his native Italy to partner with a man from Piedmont in opening a restaurant.

This was just an example. There were others. But what surprised my patient most was the spiritual similarity between the two individuals, who seemed to share the same essence, the same spirit.

To conclude the story, my patient told me that these two men had had a special meaning for him. Both had left their mark on him, or they had helped him grow: Yabricio had set the example, showing that there was no need to put off setting out to become a traveler. Paolo was the person who suggested to him that in times of need, he could ask help of the moon, and with this simple phrase, he opened for him a road to spiritual evolution.

Lastly, he told me that only one feature distinguished them: Yabricio's eyes were green and yellow. Paolo's were sky blue.

And thus Elvio concluded his tedious narrative.

"So what do you think?" said Elvio, and he looked at us expectantly. Mariano started to say something, but I couldn't take any more.

"I'm sorry," I interrupted, "I don't mean to be rude, but I really have other things on my mind at the moment. Elvio, could you please tell me where I can find Natasha?"

"Sure," said Elvio, somewhat surprised, "I didn't realize you were in such a hurry. She's going to be at the café Van Gogh right at five. She's meeting up with her girlfriends there. Is something wrong?"

"No, nothing's wrong," I said immediately. I didn't dare confess the uncontrollable storm that was being unleashed inside of me.

Then I stood up and, with a slight hesitation, I went up to him and stood looking at his cup of tea. He looked at me without saying anything. Then I leaned down and tried to bring my nose close to the teacup.

"What are you doing?" Elvio said to me.

"I want to smell your tea."

"It's not tea," he said. "It's brandy."

I left the house and began to walk hurriedly, even though I had enough time to get to the café Van Gogh before five. It was four, and I only had to walk about fifteen blocks.

I was incredibly excited by the knowledge that in just an hour I would be able to see Natasha and clear up this horrible confusion, but then I felt incredibly irritated at the fact that Elvio had gone on for so long with his absurd account. It would have taken only a few seconds to give me the information I needed, and I wouldn't have had to listen to his idiotic story. I knew two things about Elvio. One was that he was an avid reader of weird fiction. The other was that he was a liar.

Surely he had been reading *William Wilson* or *The Portrait of Dorian Grey,* and now he was trying to convince us that this fantasy of a double was something real that normally occurs in the world. I wonder how idiotic he must think we are. But anyway. None of that mattered. The only thing that mattered in that moment was to clear up this business with Natasha. And while I was thinking about this, I saw her walking ahead of me on the other side of the street. My heart jumped in my chest and I shouted her name. She didn't turn around, so I ran to her and put my hand on her shoulder.

"Natasha," I said.

But when she turned around, I realized with a start that it wasn't her. Not only that, but it really didn't look like her at all. I apologized and continued walking. This was happening to me constantly. Ever since I found out about this whole thing, I had been seeing Natasha everywhere.

I was near the café now. In no time, this unspeakable hell that was tearing at my insides would be over. Because I knew that she would tell me it wasn't true, that none of that had happened.

If it was a fling, I could understand. After all, she's as human as I, and when I had that little summer dalliance, she was understanding and forgave me. I too could forgive her if it was something like that, but this abomination? It couldn't be true.

I arrived at the café about ten minutes before five, and I stood waiting at the door. I was glad to be able to count on Natasha's punctuality, which never failed.

Those ten minutes seemed like an ocean of time. So to pass the time, I started watching the cars that stopped at the light on the corner. A rather dull diversion, but anything to distract me was a relief. Then I saw her car coming down the street the café was on. Yes, it was her new car. However, it wasn't a bright blue like Elvio had said, but rather a greenish color. But it was her. I could see her clearly, with her wavy chestnut hair and her immense smile.

But who was this guy with her? I had never seen him before.

Then the car drew closer to the café, but it didn't slow down. It just kept going and only stopped at the corner because the light was red.

I felt an intense pain go through me, the coals flaring up once more. What was going on?

I ran to the car. The window on the right side was down. Completely disregarding the passenger, I spoke to Natasha.

Only it wasn't her. Once again my imagination and conflicted emotions had gotten the best of me. This woman hardly bore any resemblance to Natasha.

Then, for the first time, I laid my eyes on the man, who was looking at me in utter amazement. In his face I saw something that I wasn't prepared for. I saw his eyes, his nose and forehead, the shape of his lips and chin. I also saw the deep scar beneath his left eye, the wrinkles in his brow. Then I saw his expression, a distinctive way of opening his eyelids, revealing surprise in a fashion I had only known in one other person in the world.

All these details I observed in a single instant, and in that terrifying moment I believed I was standing in front of an impossible mirror. Except for the vaguely lighter color of his hair, I found myself face-to-face with a perfect replica of myself.

North Shore, Oahu, February 2017

ASHES IN THE WIND

I WALKED slowly and cautiously now. The damp of the rain had mixed with the sweat of my body, so I took a minute to slow my breathing and contemplate the course of events of this still young evening. I took a few steps beyond the altar and, down to the left, I found the secret compartment. I opened it. I took out the lethal dagger I had brought with me from amongst my wet clothes, and I contemplated it for a moment. I used my shirt to clean the traces of blood that still adorned the blade, and I admired the decoration on the hilt. For a moment I held it and, with a sort of fascination, felt its weight in my hands. Then I placed it on the little cushion where it would comfortably lie. I closed the secret compartment and stood up.

I left the small building and faced the blackness of the night once more. The rain had stopped, but the air was still damp and cool. The moon was rising high and shining through the few clouds in the sky. I thought to myself that the moon knew what would take place this tragic night. As a solitary, lucid observer, it had witnessed its events, and I felt protected by its distant silence and its radiance. The gentle movement of the air brought with it an optimism or the promise of future victories. I felt encouraged and revitalized. I had much of the night ahead of me, and I felt the urge to relax for a moment. But there were still important things to be done in the course of this fateful night before I could relax or feel victorious. Danger was still lurking, and dark forces were hiding in the shadows.

I remembered my wife, who was waiting for me in her hiding place, with no news, not knowing what tragic things had happened tonight, not knowing if I was still alive. I thought about her, and I didn't want to delay my arrival and prolong her uncertainty, so I took in a huge breath of the fresh air and set off again.

I walked the dark streets, enthusiastic. I could almost feel our victory, but the moon was moving across the sky, and though the night seemed as endless as the waves of the sea, there was no time to waste. Every step of the ritual needed to be completed before the clarity of the coming day would illuminate the horizon. Nevertheless, I could sense our victory, and I thought it would be reasonable to take a minute and start to celebrate, but with a bit of willpower, I forced myself to set this idea aside and continue on.

My next destination was the hall where the folders containing our names and the rest of our information were kept and hidden, along with that of so many other unfortunate souls: men and women lost to grace and good things. As I walked through the dark streets, I was seduced by a force that led me to pause and admire the beauty of the night that surrounded me, the stealthy transit of the moon across the sky, and the musical sounds in the gloom that celebrated our next triumph. This combination of events, these gentle gifts of the night, left me feeling possessed and sedated; they invited me to rest and contemplation.

Possessed by this soothing aura, I sat down on the damp sidewalk and decided to rest. For a moment I felt exhausted and weak; for an instant I thought about sleeping. I leaned my head against the wall and closed my eyes for a few minutes. Then the clouds retreated, the moonlight hit my eyelids like a hammer and, with a start, I opened my eyes. My heart beat with fright. I could feel that my face was moist with perspiration. I was overcome with shock and fear.

How could I have dozed off? How could I have done that? If I had fallen asleep and the morning light had found me in that corner, it would have been the end of us, the end of our path.

But it wasn't. The brightness of the moon woke me and brought me back out of the trance, beating down on my eyes with her light. I stood up. I raised my eyes toward my astral protector. I was deeply grateful and, with determination, I prepared to continue on my way. I was relieved, but also frightened at the thought that, if my dream had gone on, it would have turned into an atrocious nightmare. What dark force moved me to close my eyes and rest? What dark power meant to stop me?

Resolutely and without delay I set off again. I walked down each of the streets that stood between me and my destination. I found the building and got in easily. I walked down the halls and found the door I was looking for. I tried the doorknob. Surprised and relieved, I noticed that it turned gently, and the door began to open. Once again, I felt the joyful triumph that drew yet nearer, almost tangible now. Before long all this would be over, and then I could reunite with my wife and celebrate our success.

I now found myself in the room that contained the files and the secret information. Ours would soon be destroyed. Then I needed to go to the library and read out loud from the strange volume the appointed words, those words of horror. I was supposed to do this at night and with witnesses, but that would be later. Now I had to take care of finding our files among the countless others overflowing this compartment. Fortunately, this was an easy task, as the files were meticulously organized, and it took me no more than a moment to find ours. I put them in the trash can and set them on fire. I fed the flames with a sense of satisfaction; I watched them burn, watched the red flames consume them. I breathed a deep sigh of relief, but then I noticed the large number of folders that were still left in that sinister place, and for a moment I hesitated. Then I went through the shelves again and grabbed several more files, those belonging to the people closest to us. One by one I offered them up to the fire and watched them burn up. Relieved, I watched them until there was nothing left but ashes. Gradually the fire subsided, then it wavered and was completely extinguished.

I was driven by an excitement and a determination. We were almost safe now, but what would become of them, of all these unfortunate souls whose names would still be filed in this place? I hesitated still, but a wild conviction burst forth inside of me. Why burn just a handful of these records, when a total and devastating conflagration could be unleashed? I felt an impulse coming over me; I was possessed by a clear resolution. Most of the night was still ahead of me, but the moon continued her way across the damp, dark sky. I could take the necessary time to carry out this new plan, but I ought not take too long. I quickly scattered on the floor a good number of the files that made up the huge archive, covered them with the fuel that I found on hand, and set the paper aflame; it burned, the fire spread, and very soon it engulfed and consumed everything as I was walked away down the damp and silent streets, full of joy and an extraordinary feeling of triumph.

I knew I still had time. I was brimming with an enthusiasm that propelled me down the avenues. For a moment I stopped and turned on my heels. With enormous pleasure I watched the flames rising to the sky and ravaging that abominable building, consuming each of those folders, the ashes scattered by the wind blowing about on the hot air.

I turned back around and kept walking. Once again, I felt that victory was close. Only one last step had to be taken to complete the ritual. I had to find the book containing the appointed words and speak them aloud into the night. Those painful words full of horror and suffering. I would soon find them. I was overcome with an old fear when I thought about them, but I felt encouraged by the nearness of our success and emboldened to continue on with the deed.

My next destination was the sacred building and its secret library. I had obtained the information needed to enter and the exact location of the book I was looking for. I wonder if perhaps humanity suspected the horrors that these words had scattered over the earth, the suffering and weeping that had emanated from them, the torture and horrors for which they were responsible. These words would be spoken tonight, and thus its evil power, at least for us, would come to an end. But to achieve this I had to walk the deserted streets until I found the building I was looking for.

The moon followed me, accompanying me with her brightness. I felt the shelter of her light. I walked calmly on without rushing. As if guided by some power, I once more felt the urge to rest, to relax for a while. My running turned to a slow walk and then a leisurely amble. I stopped for a moment, and my eyes were heavy, overwhelmingly burdened by a sudden sleepiness. I found it impossible to hold back the urge to sit on the sidewalk and lean my head against a wall. The fatigue was like a crushing weight upon me. I thought about dozing, and sleep washed over me like a sudden tide. I closed my eyes, and maybe I slept for a moment.

Then a rumble in the sky suddenly brought me back to consciousness. A scream from the heavens suddenly woke me. I realized that the thunder and lightning heralded the next storm, and I prepared for another downpour.

But when I raised my eyes to the sky, I was surprised to find that there were no clouds, only the moon that, like a friend, was smiling down at me. I knew then that I could no longer delay. I had to continue with the task until it was finished. I came to the street and the building I was looking for. I entered without difficulty. I walked down the halls and found the library, where I hesitated before going in. I finally pulled the bolt aside and entered the room. The pleasant smell of books came flooding out like a fresh breeze.

I set off immediately. I checked the shelves and quite easily, as if guided by a friendly hand, I found the tome I was looking for. I held it in my hands, contemplated it for a moment, and felt the pleasing texture of the cover. I had the book in my possession. I was almost done with all this.

I read the title, and to my surprise, I discovered that it was a work of literature, which had been disfigured and perverted with the purpose of bringing pain to the earth. I wondered with what regret Arthur Machen would have discovered the pernicious meaning that had been given to his words, the horrendous misrepresentation that had been derived from their meaning. I thought, in turn, if on the contrary, this might have brought him a certain delight.

I found the pages I was looking for. I decided to read them, but I didn't want to take too long. I thought about taking the book with me, but it wasn't necessary. I just needed two of the pages. I thought about tearing them out, and then about the unforgivable crime of mutilating a book. For a moment I hesitated. Then I decided that it would be permissible to take those pages out. Not only would it be permissible, but it would be an act of generosity, an incentive to the development of the imagination of its readers since, knowing the previous and subsequent pages, they would be forced to imagine for themselves the missing events. Convinced that I was acting benevolently, I tore out the pages and put them in my pocket, and then I ran from that place inhabited by books and fantasies.

I was on the street again, and I had the words with me in my pocket. I just had to recite them into the night, but I needed witnesses, and the place was deserted. I raised my eyes to the sky once more. Unsurprisingly, I found the radiant face of the moon. I thought to myself that she had witnessed every event of this singular night. She could also be the witness to these words that I needed to recite.

Then I heard a faint sound coming from a corner and noticed among the garbage on the sidewalk the presence of a friendly rodent moving among the scraps of food. I also saw, running along the tiled sidewalk, a cockroach that approached my feet, audacious and without fear. I decided that I had sufficient witnesses. I unfolded the pages I had in my pocket and held them in my hands without reading them. A moment passed. The gentle breeze dried the perspiration from my face, and the wind carried away the few clouds in the sky.

Before long, the task was through. The moon shone, triumphant, my witnesses were lost among the garbage on the sidewalk, and the tragic words had been uttered.

In that moment, I felt suddenly lighter, as if released of a burden. I also felt a renewed energy; I felt all the fatigue that was weighing me down dissipate. Recovered, and as if guided by a spirit, I set off toward my wife's hiding place, exalted by an irrepressible joy. We had succeeded!

I arrived at her shelter. I made the secret knock that we had agreed upon. She opened the door immediately and looked at me with a relief and happiness that shone in her eyes. She knew that my mere presence signified our victory.

She embraced me with a strength that I hadn't known in her. Then she stepped back from me and, holding my arms in her hands, asked me impatiently the questions quivering on her lips:

"How did things turn out?"

"Wonderfully," I replied.

"What happened to Alfredo ... is he ..." For a moment she hesitated, and I could see a deep sadness on her face. "Is he dead?"

"As far as I know Alfredo always was dead."

"And that insane amount of money? What happened to it?"

"It ended up where it belonged, in the place it never should have left.

"And the files, those cursed files?"

"They've been reduced to ashes that are floating in the wind as we speak." I could see the satisfaction and great relief on her face.

"What happened to the sorcerer?" she asked me then.

"He can't work his magic anymore. At least not on us."

"And what happened to...?" Here she cut herself off and looked at me with longing in her eyes, with an irrepressible impatience and great pain.

"What happened to the master?" she finally asked me.

"He is no longer such," I answered, relieved and triumphant.

"So we're...?"

"We're free."

Waikiki, April 2017

AS THE TRAIN PULLED AWAY I SAW HER

I ALWAYS took immense pleasure in riding the train to the last station on its route and enjoying the view of the open fields and the red autumn groves. We would then approach the cities and gradually encounter the comings and goings of people and vehicles, to finally join them and be, for a moment, part of the crowd and the commotion; then we would leave them behind and return again to the countryside, to the enormous sun that spills across the sky.

It was also a great pleasure to always travel on the window side and witness the things that happened outside of the moving train. So today, once again, I dedicated myself to this enjoyable pastime, and with the expectation of having a pleasant afternoon, I bought a ticket to the last city on the line. As usual, I sat down in one of the seats on the right-hand side of the train as it started moving, and thus began my entertainment.

Soon the train reached cruising speed, and the landscape raced by, but it allowed me to appreciate the mundane scenes: the cars that were stopped at the railroad crossings offered very little interest, except when some small incident occurred, and then the drivers would get wrapped up in some heated argument, their deplorable manners and their less appropriate vocabulary on full display. These kinds of situations always made me smile.

The spectacle I most enjoyed, however, was always that of the diversity of the colors and shapes of the trees. I could never grow tired of admiring the oaks, the monkey puzzle trees, the camphors; all the trees were a joy for me. There is no greater pleasure on earth than that of the nearness and friendship of trees.

On the other hand, coming into the cities, I also enjoyed the architecture. The orange roofs of the simple houses, the columns and domes of temples, the Gothic appearance of the stone houses. All these ordinary things were the joy of traveling by train for me.

None of these were what most caught my attention today however, because a funny thing occurred. It happened that, as the train was speeding up as it left one of the stations, my eyes were captivated by the singular beauty of a tall and strikingly attractive woman. Her hair was long and black, and it shone like the stars. Her lips, red as blood, suggested the promise of a nameless passion.

The train had already reached a considerable speed, and although I saw her only for a moment, her image was burned into my mind, and as the train pulled away, I turned my head to get another look at this creature of singular beauty. Then something unusual and surprising happened: she turned her eyes towards me, violently piercing mine, revealing a perverse fervor from which I had to avert my eyes, and her red lips formed a smile that held no semblance of tenderness, but rather of something dark and sinister, like something dead.

I was amazed by the response of this strange woman, and I immediately looked at the seat in front of me to distract myself from this astonishing sight. For a moment I didn't dare look out the window again, and I took a few minutes to meditate on what had happened. I couldn't understand how it was possible that this woman knew that I was looking at her, when she was so far away from the moving train. I was disturbed by the precision with which her eyes fixed on mine, and much more by her expression, her chilling smile, combined with a gaze that seemed to know me and see right through me.

How did this woman know that I was following her with my eyes? How could she return my gaze so precisely, so piercingly?

Yet what was most unsettling, most disturbing about this uncanny experience was the response within me, the impact of her dark eyes upon my soul, for her beauty made me shudder, and at the same time a chill ran through my body as I felt her penetrating gaze, and suddenly I knew that this woman had worked a dark power in me. What was this gloomy and perverse quality that she had?

I was thinking all these things as the train left the scene, continuing on its way, and I was relieved to put distance between me and that unsettling woman. But I dared not look out the window again for a moment, and I was content to watch the people who were boarding the train through the door ahead of me: a bald man and an overweight woman in an elegant dress, followed by a boy with his mother and a gentleman in slovenly clothes.

It seemed to me that the spectacle on display inside the train couldn't compare with the one unfolding outside. At least that was what I thought until the same door that opened for those lackluster characters also opened, unexpectedly, for that disturbing woman, who I had seen a few minutes earlier on a sidewalk, far off in the distance outside the train. The shock and alarm were doubtless written on my face, because the strange woman immediately fixed her eyes on mine, as she had done before, filling me with an indescribable dread.

How was it possible that she was inside the car and, to my astonishment, walking towards me?

She managed to read these thoughts in my eyes, for her sensual lips transformed into a horrendous smile, as her eyes expressed a joy that fed on my confusion and my fear, which intensified as she drew closer.

There was something dark in her face, in her glance, something perhaps inhuman that I couldn't bear, so I looked down at my shoes as she continued walking towards me, and as she passed me by, I felt her black eyes fixate on me; a shudder ran under my skin, and a cold dread penetrated to my bones.

Without a doubt, something dark and sinister was lurking inside this strange woman. But she passed me and then moved away, continued walking, and perhaps sat down in the next car. I tried to calm my emotions and divert my thoughts, but it was impossible for me to shake the impression of this stunning apparition and the terror instilled in me by the expression of her face and her irresistible nearness.

I returned my attention to the window, hoping to find some distraction in the landscape that would take away the images of that woman, but from the turbulent emotions that agitated me, I found no rest in the jovial crowds of the streets, nor in the stone architecture, nor in the brightness of the sun bouncing off the leaves on the trees.

With this oppressive weight pushing down on me, I sought refuge in the sleep that would undoubtedly take me away from that woman, from the pain that represented the persistence of her image in my eyes, from her sensual red lips, from the indescribable restlessness that burned me like fire when I thought of her. Then I closed my eyes and gave in to sleep, a gentle relief, which brought me to sweet, soft places where I was comfortable; I forgot my sorrows and felt warm and protected like a child in his mother's arms. I rested like this for a what seemed forever; I stayed in those mother's arms that embraced me, encircled me, and when I felt hungry I found her fertile and naked breasts, so I drank from them and fed until I was satiated, so that when I was satisfied, I opened my childlike oneiric eyes to see the face of this diligent mother who cared for me and fed me, and it was with the utmost horror that I looked up to see the hideous face of the woman I feared, to see her exquisite lips and her sensual gaze. With a scream I awoke from my horrendous dream. My body oozed with sticky sweat, and my heart beat in my chest like a drum. I was overwhelmed and terrified. I needed to escape; I had to leave or hide. I thought that she might still be on this infernal train, and I felt the irrepressible need to get off, to walk the streets so that the fresh air would disperse these shadows that were closing in on me. Relieved, I noticed that the train was slowing down as it approached the next city and the next stop. Soon I would get off and get away from this whole strange nightmare.

The train stopped. Without a moment's delay, I got off and hurried down the platform through the crowd of people. I left the station and disappeared among the streets. I didn't know what city I was in, but it was a joy to no longer be in that cursed train car, and I breathed a sigh of relief to know that as the train was leaving, that woman was getting farther away and disappearing.

Walking down the verdant avenues of that city, my heart finally came down to its usual rhythm, and my hurried steps slowed to a walk as I gained control of my emotions; my mind found rest in the contemplation of the arts and crafts displayed for sale on the pedestrian street I walked along, where the various shops advertised their wares. I found well-designed porcelain with cheerful and colorful images, bracelets and rings, artistic and extravagant images.

I kept walking and enjoyed this little strip of shops, a pleasant distraction for me. The next storefront displayed paintings and frames for photographs, some simple and restrained, others highly decorated, extravagant, and baroque. My attention suddenly focused on the images of the people in the portrait holders on display in the shop window. Happy families and smiling people, children with their parents, and others in the company of dogs or cats. Then, with unspeakable surprise, I found among the images of these characters the terrifying face that I feared, the perverse smile on her perfect lips that burned fiery red, the beastly eyes, the perfect pallor of her skin that was white as death, the malevolent expression in those persistent eyes that seemed to follow me from the printed paper of the photo—eyes that seemed alive.

How was it possible? How could those paper eyes be fixated on mine, scrutinizing me to my core and filling me with this paralyzing panic? How was it possible? There was no way to know, but I managed to run down the cobblestone street away from the store, and from the terror that her evil glance instilled in my soul.

I don›t know how many streets I ran down or how many corners I turned, but when my gait relaxed and I was too exhausted to go on, I found myself in an alley that led to the entrance of a temple that, though it held nothing of the extraordinary, seemed immense in its kindness and protection.

Without a moment's hesitation, I went in, and walked down the center aisle between the rows of pews. I contemplated the holy images and the luminous candles. I felt the shelter of this warm and protective environment. I didn't know until that moment how much I believed in God and all the saints. I bowed down, prayed, beseeched the help of the light; I begged for divine assistance, and several minutes, maybe a few hours passed. Time became a vague notion as I regained my strength and sanity. I finally felt revitalized, renewed by rest and prayer, possessed of my strength again.

It was thus that I reasoned that all these unusual events of the day were nothing more than a rare succession of coincidences that had unfavorably piled up in my consciousness to generate this paranoia that now gripped me. I knew there was nothing to fear except my silly superstition and my excitable imagination. I also knew that some divine force had clarified my understanding and had removed my childish phantasmagorias. I felt that renewing presence coming to me from above, from the light, to protect and encompass me, so that any dark influence would be completely rejected. Thus, revived and recovered, I prepared to leave the building and return to the streets to take the train once more and return home.

I walked the steps that lay between me and the entrance of the temple, and when I reached the door, I opened it decisively, and when I took my first step onto the sidewalk, I was struck by the most paralyzing terror upon finding the horrendous woman that I feared, the demon in front of me.

Her eyes, black as hatred, struck me with an impossible fervor. Her silky long hair and perfect skin made my head swim; her terrible, sensual lips ceased their mocking smile and opened slowly as she uttered these words:

"There's no point in running or hiding. You are already mine."

Cordova, Alaska, July 2017

THE LOST CHILD

THE afternoon was drawing nearer to its end and the sun to the horizon. I grabbed the leash and collar and got myself ready to take a short walk with Canelita as far as the gate to enjoy this lovely time of day together.

Canela loves our walks and trotted along to the gate with me, all obedient delight as usual, where we sat at the foot of one of the pines that form a kind of gateway to the Garzarelli farm. We made ourselves comfortable and settled down to contemplate the evening. Canela rolled onto her back for me to scratch her belly and, unsurprised, I noticed that her smile was like the rebound of the sun off the needles of the pine trees and that the pinks and oranges lining the clouds were reflected in the eyes of my beloved companion.

We relaxed and relished these happy moments of the evening as the sun disappeared completely, and the light became a faint pale phosphorescence on the horizon. The early evening held onto the warmth of the afternoon, so we enjoyed staying on a while longer, Canela and I, sitting on the ground enjoying the breeze, which brought the scents of the sown field and the music of the wind in the trees.

The light of day finally died and, meekly, one by one, the stars began to populate the sky. The night was now black and serene; the stars had completely flooded the sky. Then, to our complete surprise, and from one moment to the next, a continuous blinding light appeared over the field a few dozen yards away from the spot where Canela and I were still sitting.

Where this unexpected light came from was a mystery to me. But more mysterious was that it seemed to possess a life of its own, for at times it would weaken, then regain its brilliance, while appearing to move first sideways and then slightly upwards until, suddenly, as unexpectedly as it had appeared, it went out in a single moment and vanished without a trace.

As this strange light illuminated the sky, Canela reacted by jumping to her feet with a gruff bark and sped off in the direction of the house. For a moment, I stood there feeling slightly dazed, not just at the strangeness of the event, but far more at the odd sensation that witnessing it had left me with. I felt surprised, but frightened too, as if that light concealed something sinister, and a premonition of dark things took hold of me as a shudder ran through my body.

But Canela had run off and I wanted to find her. So, I returned to the house, and I quickened my pace to get away from the spot where I had seen that weird light as soon as possible.

I thought I would find Canela at the kitchen door, waiting to get into the house, but the door was open, and there was no sign of her. After having a glass of water and preparing some food for Canela and myself, I went to my room in the certainty she would be waiting for me on the bed, comfortably spread out on the sheets, as usual, drooling on the pillow and covering everything with hair; as usual, in other words, smiling and happy. But when I got to my room, she wasn't there. With growing concern, I thought about going to look for her as I sat on the bed, when a sudden fatigue knocked me flat on the bed, and sleep flooded over me. As my eyes closed, I hoped that tomorrow Canela would be back with me on the bed, licking my feet to wake me up.

That night, I had trouble sleeping and was woken repeatedly by turbulent dreams. By the morning, I felt quite tired. Try as I might, I was unable to recall the haunting images that had hounded me in the night and plunged me as I slept into some dark place which, even after waking, and in the clear light of day, I had not succeeded in leaving.

To my great surprise, I realized that Canela wasn't in the bedroom, which was very strange, for she was a dog who would never leave me to sleep alone. I went to the kitchen, but she wasn't there, and then I checked every room in the house only to feel a sinking disappointment. I couldn't find her anywhere. I left the main building and, shouting her name, I first checked the raspberry field and then the orchard where the peaches grow, fully expecting to find her there, smiling and wagging her tail back and forth and overjoyed to see me. But I found nothing other than the disappointment of her absence and the disquieting feeling of being enveloped by something dark and painful.

I continued along the lane to the staff quarters, shouting my beloved dog's name at the top of my lungs, and advanced along the gravel path, sinking further with every step into a murky slick of unease and concern. But this uncertainty did not reach its peak until I came to the staff house and heard, through the open dining room window, the conversation that Jarvis, the caretaker, was having with his wife.

"We have to leave," she said.

"Matilde, are you crazy? Here we have work, food, a roof over our heads. What do you mean 'leave'? Where to?"

"Don't you worry about that," said Matilde. "This place is doomed, you'll see. And we have to get out of here before anything happens to us, my dear husband; we have to get out of here as soon as we can."

"But Matilde, what will we do?"

"It doesn't matter, dear, it doesn't matter! You seen it. You seen the Bad Light. Bad things are coming our way, dear! We have to leave this place."

That was all I could glean before turning on my heels and retracing my steps, this time with a shudder running through my body as, for the first time since the event, I recalled the odd light of the previous day.

By noon my confusion had become consternation, for Canela was still nowhere to be found.

Unexpectedly, Jarvis appeared in the kitchen, where I was sipping hot maté. He had his cap in his hands and was wringing it continuously in great agitation. I invited him to sit, but he preferred to stand and told me that he could no longer work on the estate, that he had to leave before the day was out. Upon asking him why he had made such a drastic decision, his eyes sank floorward, and he fell silent. After a moment, he looked up and said, in clear trepidation, that he could give me no explanation, but that he had to leave as soon as possible. So he held out a trembling hand, which I shook firmly, and he took his leave, plunging me ever deeper into uncertainty. What sudden transformation was taking place in this house? I thought for a moment, as the memory of the horrid light and its poisonous sheen from the night before flooded back to me.

The next day witnessed the occurrence that filled the peaceful afternoons in our country house with horror.

I spotted Gandolfo coming through the entrance gate and approaching the house with some haste while staring at a bundle cradled in his arms. I watched him drawing nearer and realized he was talking to the bundle he was carrying, which seemed to be wriggling. When he was close enough, I noticed it was a baby he was holding, and that it took up his full attention.

As he walked past me, and without diverting his gaze from the child for a second, he said: "I found this baby out in the wheatfields." A sudden intuition warned me not to look, not to set eyes on the child my friend had brought. Yet, in my state of shock, I got up at once and looked at the child. Immediately, I had to turn away, for this creature met my gaze, fixing his eyes on mine in a strange, disturbing way.

There was something unpleasant in his eyes. And something ancient. As if it were the gaze of an old man, an aged man, anything but an infant. This first impression made me promptly recoil, and somehow, I knew that if I had continued to look into them, those eyes would have seduced me sweetly, like sunlight reflecting off ears of wheat. There was something dreadfully magnetic in them, something irresistible that drew in one's eyes. I immediately backed away from both of them, and an inner voice told me never to go anywhere near them again.

And so it was that this child of woe joined our unhappy abode.

The series of events that followed, I can only recall in blurs and fragments. Perhaps all the might of my being is trying to keep them at bay, to erase them. Gandolfo developed an automatic and disproportionate fondness for the child. I found it very strange that his behavior had been transformed almost instantly and that he had begun to act entirely out of character. His habits changed overnight. He would do nothing but go to bizarre and excessive lengths to indulge this child.

One afternoon, when I gloomily returned from an unsuccessful search for Canela in the neighboring fields, I came across Gandolfo having an animated conversation with someone who had to be very close but whom I could not see. When he turned, I realized with paralyzing surprise that the person he was conversing with was this peculiar child he carried around in his arms, who was muttering words into his ears that I couldn't hear, but that would have been impossible for a child of that age and development to pronounce.

Even more disturbing was the change in Gandolfo's expressions, which flitted between a macabre smile one moment and the deepest, most painful sorrow the next. Then, with a single movement of his body, Gandolfo allowed me to see the face of this bizarre child. Intimidated by the memory of his magnetic eyes, I immediately looked away and hurried off from the disturbing scene.

It was the last time I ever saw Gandolfo on the farm. He never said goodbye; he didn't say anything before he left. He simply disappeared. The boy, however, remained with us. It was the Lizaldre sisters who took Gandolfo's place in caring for this strange child whose proximity I found so unbearable. They looked after him with the same devotion as Gandolfo had, and I had the distinct impression that this baby was becoming the very epicenter of their attention.

One sad, gray afternoon, I found Julieta alone in the kitchen and seized the opportunity to ask her about Gandolfo's sudden absence. She put down the slice of bread with which she was making a sandwich and, taking a knife firmly in her right hand, she squeezed it until her veins swelled as she stood there before me with a menacing glint in her eyes as she told me that our friend had taken his car into town to be fixed by a mechanic.

Two things struck me as utterly peculiar. The first was the oddity of Julieta's manners, the wildness in her eyes: her expression revealed a profound change that had taken place in her personality over just a few days. I could not put my finger on the exact nature of this transformation, yet it was extremely evident nonetheless: the energy emanating from her, accompanied by her gaze and her movements, were those of an entirely different person.

The second peculiar thing was the simple fact that Gandolfo's vehicle had been parked in the garage for days.

After this brief encounter with Julieta, events at home took a fairly normal course until the terrible night when a ghastly dread filled every living cell in my trembling body, the night I had to flee from that accursed house.

Nightfall blackened the land and the lusterless stars refused to light my soul, which was dark as the night itself. Such was the influence on it of recent events, which had plunged me into a sea of uncertainty over the loss of my beloved dog and all the outlandish things that came after.

As I said, the night was black, and black too was the house in the wee small hours, when I was woken by screaming and sobbing coming from the sisters' room. For a moment I lay there in bed, expectant and curious, taken aback by the array of sounds coming from their room, a mixture of mocking laughter, cackling, and shrieks of pain.

I got out of bed and left my room. I walked down the hall to the sisters' room, determined to find out what was going on. I stood outside the door and reached out to turn the doorknob but was stopped short by a sound from within. It was a deep, gruff voice, like a grown man's and, though I couldn't understand the language it was speaking, it was clearly giving commands, answered now with shrieks of appalling torment, now with the sound of laughter which rose at intervals to a hideous cackle.

I hesitated for a moment. My resolve to turn the doorknob, open the door, and find out just what scene was playing out inside suddenly became a paralyzing dread, not only from the maniacal sounds issuing from the room, but far more because they suddenly stopped the moment my hand touched the doorknob.

I realized that, whoever they were, the people inside the room knew I was on the other side of the door. So, for a silent moment that felt like an eternity, I stood there, frozen to the spot, hesitant and sweating, fighting to retain my wits and soundness of mind.

Another event brought me back from my trance. From inside the room came the patter of quick little footsteps hurrying toward the door. There was something quite uncanny about this new sound: the fact that the steps sounded as firm and heavy as would those of an adult, but close together as would those of a child with very short legs. Like a baby's.

I suddenly felt in full possession of my faculties. I ran to my room, bolted the door, turned off the light, and hid under the covers. For a moment, I heard nothing but silence. But then the terror reached my ears in the form of that heavy patter I had heard moments before inside the sisters' room. Again, I was paralyzed by panic. My soul was ice, and I felt alone and helpless.

This turbulence in my soul lasted an incalculable length of time, or perhaps it was the plan of time, in its malice, to come to a stop, prolonging my horror and despair. Then a different sound made me aware that time was still passing. I heard the doorknob turn, followed by a soft but deliberate attempt to open my bedroom door, but it was locked, and that brought me relief and a sense of security.

I was then completely overwhelmed by a new wave of terror, for I thought I could see the child's silhouette inside the room, inside my room. I closed my eyes, my body paralyzed and possessed by terror, and gave myself up completely to divine protection. The insidious minutes seemed endless and elastic, the hours were centuries.

It finally dawned on me that some black magic had been worked upon time itself, and time, in service of the shadows, had stopped in order to perpetuate my horror so that I would remain in this permanent state of incalculable anguish.

And so, when I saw through the window a light in the east and glimpsed the first glints of dawn, my soul was released from this extraordinary burden, and I realized that time was back on course, and that what I saw beyond the window was the glow of the new day whose light and warmth would drive away this darkness that was enveloping me. I felt revived and hopeful. I dared to move for the first time and, in an act of supreme courage, I looked up to see if that dreaded child was indeed inside my room.

My spirit soared when I saw that I was the only person there. I didn't waste a second. Revived by this discovery, I was determined to get away from the estate as soon as possible. I opened the window and, with the encouraging light of day, leaped through it and ran in no particular direction, simply to put as much distance between myself and this bedeviled place as I could.

I fled through the trees. I found a trail and followed it for some time in the belief that it would lead me to the right place, far from the house I now feared so much. I felt myself guided by an impulse. I realized that my feet were following a path that had been worn by others, which seemed to be showing me the way, and I instinctively followed it without a second's thought, as if hypnotized. Step after step, I advanced along the trail, climbing a small slope. As I reached the top, my eyes met with the sight of the rising sun peeking over the horizon. Magically, its warm light shook me awake, dragging me out of that hypnotic trance into which I had somehow fallen.

I halted in my tracks, only to discover that two or three steps further on from the blessed spot where I had stopped, the incline came to an abrupt end and fell sharply away. Further below, in the deepest part of this formation, my eyes beheld a new horror when they fell upon the mutilated corpse of our friend Gandolfo.

At the bottom of this depression in the terrain were the circular blades from the sawmill. I was shocked by how meticulously these razor-sharp instruments had been laid out. They had clearly been set up in that place for the sinister purpose of mutilating our friend, and they had fulfilled their dark design most effectively. Far more, I was shocked, or terrified to see the unpredictable expression on Gandolfo's face. His head was completely separated from his body, but his face wore a smile, beaming with warmth and tenderness. What could have made Gandolfo smile, what could have pleased him so much in his final moment? Especially when it had been so brutal and horrible an end.

As the fear took hold of me, my jumbled thoughts brought back the memory of that damned child, and again I shuddered with my whole body.

I roamed the trails that awful morning until I found the one that led to the village. Wandering through the streets felt like a blessing, and treading its neat cobblestones little by little restored control of my senses. Now I was in a normal, familiar place, and the things that had happened during the night seemed remote and unreal. Strolling through the village streets and sharing them with the early risers released me from the trance I had been in, and reality recovered its proper shape and dimension.

When I saw the baker greeting his neighbor on his doorstep, when I smelled the aroma of hot fresh-baked bread, I finally felt fully awake. So, I asked the baker about the animal shelter, where I hoped I'd find Canela. I also asked him about the station and the next train away from this place, once so beloved, now stained black.

The baker answered me with a smile and another question:

"How's your day going, my good man?"

"My day isn't going at all, sir," I answered with uncharacteristic discourtesy.

I could read in his face the shock at my bad manners, so I composed myself.

"Forgive me," I said. "My day is going splendidly," I replied, this time with ironic impatience.

The man looked at me strangely and said, "Well, I'm glad. Mine is going really well, too. The birds always sing at this time of the morning."

So I mustered all my patience and followed suit. Our early morning conversation covered the most inconsequential of subjects: the variable price of flour, the moisture that accumulates at the top of the oven and, finally, to cap our verbal exchange, we discussed the rising power of fresh versus dry yeast.

I thought the day might end before this man would give me the information I needed. This bland, mundane conversation went on for minutes that felt like hours, and I feared that time itself would stop, and the two of us would be lost in some nameless place.

But then, miraculously, the man told me what I needed to know and longed for so much: he pointed the way to the animal shelter and told me there were no trains to Constitución until the next day.

Our conversation was over. I thought it had lasted longer than it takes a star to ignite fire and explode, but when I looked at my watch, I discovered it had barely been half an hour. I was glad. I walked to the animal shelter as fast as I could. It was closed, so I waited, and at the same time rested to recover the energy depleted by the events of the night before.

When the shelter finally opened again, I was overjoyed to be reunited with my beloved Canelita. She was all over me, covering me with kisses and affection. We left together and found accommodations in a boarding house that rented us a room for the night. In the morning, we took the train to Constitución. As we were waiting for the train, I heard the other passengers talking about the heinous crimes that had been committed out on the Garzarelli estate.

Following an impulse, much against my wont, I grabbed a newspaper from the news-stand and stowed it in my bag without reading a word. The train came. We got on and left.

***

Evenings followed mornings, weeks followed days. A month passed, or maybe longer. Back in my permanent house in Maine, the things that had happened in Pedernales seemed remote and unreal, like a dream. It's true that I hadn't been able to put them out of my mind, but I had succeeded in leaving them behind like a pair of worn-out old shoes. Then, by chance or the will of the universe, I found in my travel bag the newspaper I had picked up at the train station the day we left Pedernales. I opened it and leafed through, knowing that there would be something in it of interest.

I wasn't disappointed because that day's edition included an article about the strange goings-on of that fateful night. I read it eagerly. The article attempted to make sense of the discovery by the authorities of mutilated corpses that bore witness to the hideous things that took place that night on the Garzarelli estate. I won't try to

| THE LOST CHILD

reproduce the article, but I will repeat the parts that cast light on my understanding of the appalling events that played out there.

The article explained that the bodies of the Lizaldre sisters were found lifeless in one of the rooms of the house in the most bizarre of circumstances. The youngest of the sisters was found tied to one of the beds, her body lacerated from head to foot. The cuts had been made by a rather blunt instrument that had shredded her skin in a way that must have been excruciatingly painful. The forensic investigation clearly established the fact that the elder sister had been the cause of these wounds and her sister's death. The report left no doubt that having committed this atrocity, Julieta had ended her own life in the same way as she had her sister's. The article made no mention of the presence of anyone else in the room where the sinister acts had unfolded.

As for the death of Gandolfo, the newspaper mentioned that the saws that had mutilated his body had been dragged from the barn to the scene of the crime with great effort. The way these saws had been set up to fulfill their deadly purpose was proof of a careful plan executed with detail and precision. They had been placed there with the utmost care, their sharpest cutting edges exposed so that they would end the victim's life in macabre, theatrical fashion.

The piece also left no doubt that there was absolutely no evidence to suggest that Gandolfo had been forced to jump off the edge of the cliff, where death awaited him below. The evidence pointed to the fact that he had done so of his own free will. The newspaper also explained that, to succeed in completely separating the head from the body, the man would have had to leap into the abyss with pinpoint accuracy, a quite astonishing detail.

I stopped reading at that point. I understood immediately that Gandolfo had gone about preparing his death with great care, and that its execution had required great application and dedication. He had meticulously and resolutely taken his own life. Maybe that explained the expression of jubilation and triumph on his face when I found him that morning, at the bottom of the cliff, headless and smiling.

There was no mention of the presence of anyone else in the house, nor of what might have caused such horrors. It simply stated that the investigation was ongoing. I felt drained and disturbed by what I had learned from reading the article.

It became clear in my mind what had happened to Gandolfo and the Lizaldre sisters, but it deepened my confusion about the strange creature that had visited us in the form of a lost child, with his design to corrupt and ruin us. That same afternoon, I visited the Portland Public Library, where normally a pleasant atmosphere and the companionship of books awaited me. I scoured its catalogue for information on demons, Lucifers and other denizens of the darkness.

In the *Twilight Encyclopedia,* I found an article about the existence, in the South American Pampas, of a child of the darkness that takes the form of an abandoned, innocent child that allows people to approach, then corrupts their souls and destroys their bodies. The article also mentioned that, once wounded by this intruder's sadistic poison, the victim's soul plunges into a labyrinth of pain, where it is lost forever, without return or escape.

It also pointed out that merely from eye contact between demon and victim, it is enough to effect the contamination, and that the duration of this meeting of gazes determines the speed with which the spiritual poison spreads its power through the victim; after this contact, no one can escape the torment that awaits them.

I closed the book and left the library. As I trudged through the snow-covered streets, I felt that the icy climes of the northern hemisphere were in fact a warm blanket shielding me with their distance from the Argentine Pampas, which I now found so odious. I recalled with a deep sense of relief that my eyes had never met the child's, that filthy beast, and I confidently walked to my apartment, determined never to set foot on the Garzarelli farm and enter that house of horrors again.

* * *

The next few months passed like so many others. But one day, it dawned on me, to my surprise, that for a time—I found it hard to say precisely how long—I had stopped going to work. I also realized I had rarely left the bed I was lying in, and that I was finding it difficult to tell waking from sleeping. Sleep was a turbulent stream of grotesque images that assailed me at night, or in the daytime; it was hard to tell, because presently day and night had become weirdly confused and felt like an endless succession of vain hours that brought wicked thoughts and the strange portent of some future darkness or permanent pain.

I thought of Canela and her sweet smile. I tried in vain to remember the last time we had gone for a walk and wondered why she no longer came onto the bed to sleep with me. Then I saw her lying on the floor, or perhaps spread out, in a huge pool of something strange that surrounded and covered her.

My consciousness abandoned me again, as it so often did of late, and I found myself plunged once again into a whirl of sordid images, trapped by an all-conquering darkness from which I knew it would be impossible for me to escape. Eventually I awoke or came to. I tried to leave my bed and stand, only to find I no longer could. All I could do was raise my eyes, which were naturally drawn to Canela, or the mound of meat that had once been Canela. And from her corner came the stench of despair and dead things.

Honolulu, December 2017

THE GOLEM

I MAY be no rabbi, but I do possess a detailed knowledge of the subtleties and secrets of the legend. I devoted myself to the study of every particular of this delicate question with painstaking dedication. I gave myself wholeheartedly to research and reflection until I came to a full and meticulous understanding of every aspect of the labor that I intended to undertake. I set my mind to hatching the perfect plan and resolutely set about putting it into action. I traveled to Prague and found accommodations in a shabby tenement forgotten by men and abandoned by time, lost in the murky streets of this ancient city and veiled by somber trees. Far from men and concealed by shadows and indifference, my lodgings furnished me with a space perfectly suited to my need for work and seclusion.

With passion and care, love and patience, I gathered the clay from the banks of the Vltava River, whose waters bring a scent of sweetness and whose currents carry the musical murmur of justice. That was my goal: to do my utmost to attain that slippery justice that still eluded me.

With this in mind, I fashioned my child in that clay. With passion and tenderness, fervor and diligence, I formed its body and composed its face, molded its arms and legs, and gave myself to this work with the utmost devotion and most ardent zeal until my creature was finished. One last touch to its hands, another to its face, and the task was complete. For a moment, in joy and satisfaction, I contemplated the fruit of my labors, the result of so many hours of painstaking work.

I gazed at my lifeless child as it stood before me, upright like a man, with its still unbeating heart, this Golem conceived by my own hand. Then I stood back to admire the result of my efforts and bathe in the satisfaction of a mission accomplished and well executed, to wallow in the joyous knowledge that justice would, in the end, prevail, and the man responsible for my sorrow would pay.

And so, my creature of clay was begotten. I now had to wait for the favorable alignment of the constellations in order to pronounce the invocations and inflame its inert body with life. Yet I was invaded by a painful worry. My whole life had collapsed. After losing my job at the museum, my finances became a shambles and I fell headlong into the abyss of liquor. My wife, my companion of so many years, was unable to bear the ruin my life had become and finally moved away, abandoning our home and our love. She now pursues her fate who knows where, but not in our house, which has grown cold and lonely. How did it come to this? I was always thoroughgoing in my duties at the museum and devoted in my work. What did I do to lose the post which led me to this ruin?

I didn't know precisely how things had come about or what the details were, but I did have enough clues to form an inkling of the sequence of events: Arnaldo, who took my place as head of the Tibetan collection, and the director of the museum had schemed against me and hatched a devious plot to persuade the general board to remove me from my post. But whoever had executed the plan remained a mystery to me, and not knowing the true culprit of my misfortunes was a problem.

I am a good man, a fair man. I don't wish for all of them to die, just the swine to blame for my pain. But how can I know for sure who the person is that I detest?

Without that information, I shan't be able to give the Golem a precise command, and without that command, it will be unable to carry out the task it was created for.

Occupied by such thoughts, I laid my head on my pillow and, with these turbulent ideas swirling around my head, I was overtaken by slumber. In the delirium of my dreams, I found myself journeying through a scorching, suffocating desert landscape. The air boiled like a cauldron, and my bare feet suffered unspeakable torment. Thirst choked my throat, and the sun burned and blazed immutable as ever above me.

An immeasurable eternity passed like this, but eventually the vast wasteland came to an end, and suddenly I found myself in a black, desolate swamp. My path wound onward, though I had no idea where it was leading me, and the atmosphere around me radiated a gray, poisonous miasma. The stench of death hung in the air, fouling my lungs, and I found it painful to breathe.

Somehow, I knew that, while my path in this place stretched away almost to infinity, it would eventually end; I also knew that, at the end of this path, I had to traverse a place of darkness.

My dream reached its conclusion, and when I awoke, a single conviction ruled my waking mind. All of a sudden, I saw clearly the order I had to give to the Golem. I didn't need to pronounce the name of the person who was to die; I had simply to direct it to put to death whoever was truly to blame for my sorrow and pain, so the Golem would know who to kill.

I came around from my dream with a feeling of elation and triumph. Finally, I had the answer to my problem. Now all I had to do was wait for the right moment to kindle life in my clay creature.

Finally, that moment arrived. Venus entered the constellation of Libra. The stars were favorably aligned. This was the long-awaited moment.

At home, in my secret retreat, far from wagging tongues, I faced my clay child. I raised my arms aloft, pronounced the invocation, and summoned the spirits of life and death. I drew up a stepstool, so I could reach the head of this creature modeled by my own hand, and in its forehead, I traced the letters of the vital word. Then I put my lips to its ear and, slowly and carefully, whispered the words, "I want you to kill. I want you to slay the real culprit of my misery." Then I opened its mouth, and beneath its tongue, I slipped the parchment bearing the appointed words. I climbed down from the stool and stood before the Golem. For a moment, nothing happened, and everything was calm. The minutes seemed to stretch on, and still I stood in expectation before the Golem.

Then I noticed a flutter in the Golem's chest, barely perceptible, and my heart leaped inside me in accompaniment. The flutter became more rhythmic, and I no longer doubted: my child was alive. I gazed at it with love and caution, with tenderness and expectation. Then I observed a flicker of its clay eyelids, which opened to reveal the dead gaze of its clay eyes. Overcome with excitement and elation, I backed away, my eyes fixed on my living creature, until my shoulders came up against the wall.

Then the Golem began to move. Gingerly, it bent its knee and took its first step, then, with the same gingerness and caution, it took its second, and more steps followed, one after another, as it made directly for me, until its enormous body stood before my own, and, with the same caution, it raised its arms toward me, and its strong, dread hands closed on my neck and squeezed it relentlessly, turning it into a formless, dripping red mass. Its mortal hands then loosened and released my body, which crumpled, inert and lifeless, to the floor.

Cordova, Alaska, July 2017

OVER THE COURSE OF AN AFTERNOON

I ENTERED the waiting room shortly after 12:45 pm, so I arrived a little late, but it seemed like an acceptable delay. On impulse, I did a walk-around of the room, the dimensions of which surprised me, for it was a little smaller than I had imagined. The hallway brought me to the door and, once inside, I found a room with access to two others. One of them was opposite me, a little to the left, and the other was to my right. I was pleasantly surprised to find, to my left, a large window at one end of the room, across from one of the doors. I took a few steps toward the large window and went out on the balcony.

It was the beginning of the afternoon. The warm summer breeze rustled the leaves of the trees and whispered some secret for the ears of those attentive enough to listen. The sun was high, bright, and luminous. The presence of the balcony made me happy, as balconies always do, and I wondered at the strange bond between me and them that brings me a private, secret satisfaction.

I went back into the room, which was really a sort of foyer, and I was saddened by its austerity; there was only a chair in it, a small desk on top of which two shelves housed some books, and a framed picture hanging on the wall in front of the chair. I perused the books on the shelf, only to discover that there was nothing interesting, just a volume by Felisberto Hernandez, one by Kafka, another by Edgar Allan Poe, and one more by an unknown author. After conducting a brief inspection, I found that was all there was in the place. So I took a seat and prepared myself to wait.

As often happens in these circumstances, it seemed to me that the time passed very slowly. To entertain myself, I turned my attention to the little painting that was on the wall right across from me. It portrayed a curious and rather singular image, but it held my attention only for a moment. What could I do now but wait and allow my eyes to wander? The minutes seemed like hours, the seconds seemed without limit or end. I was agitated at finding myself in this room with nothing to do and nothing to entertain myself with, so I went back to looking out the window at the sun, watching it make its way across the sky. It was then that the scene around me changed for the first time. I heard footsteps in the room to my right, of people who seemed, judging by the sound of the chairs, to be sitting down around a table and making themselves comfortable. This minor commotion lasted only a moment, after which I sensed that every person in the room had found their place and sat down. Then I noticed a glow coming from that room, as that of candlelight would be, and a glittering orange could be seen through the door, which was slightly ajar, allowing the passage of the warm reddish light and the sound of the people.

I was thoroughly surprised to find that, almost at the same moment that the candle or candelabra was lit in the room to my right, an electric light in the room across from me came on in answer. I didn't know until that moment that there was anyone in that room, because it had been quiet, and the door was closed. Soon after, in the room to my right, calmly and slowly, I began to hear a murmur, as if the attendees of that gathering were engaged in the intense discussion of an important matter. What they were saying was incomprehensible to me, but I discerned that they were speaking about a sensitive subject, and this murmuring went on for some time; how long, I can't be sure.

Meanwhile, as soon as the talking started in the room to my right, there began a low, sad sobbing in the room across from me. That is, a soft crying, but pained and constant. I was struck with utter amazement and curiosity. What was going on in this place? What strange ceremony was taking place in the room next to me, and what was its connection to what was happening in the other one? My curiosity bubbled forth, like a spring that's begun to trickle but cannot stop. The murmuring and crying went on for an indefinite period of time. Perhaps it was an hour, or maybe endless minutes. After a while, the murmuring or the conversation suddenly stopped, and the glow of the candle decreased in intensity. Almost in unison, the crying from the room across from me also came to an end, and there was a moment of calm. I couldn't hear anything from one room or the other. As if of a mutual accord, the two places surrendered to the silence or resigned themselves to secrecy and stillness, so that I once again found myself surrounded by serenity and boredom.

However, this time my senses were focused on the memory of the strange things that were happening. What was the meaning of the events that were unfolding around me? My curiosity grew like an unstoppable deluge.

Once again, I looked for something to distract myself. Then I realized, surprised and bewildered, that a birdcage occupied a corner of the little enclosure where I found myself, suspended in the air, hanging from the ceiling and trapping those unfortunate creatures inside: a cage that until that moment I hadn't seen. Without a moment's hesitation, I jumped swiftly to my feet and walked up to the hanging prison. I stood in front of it and contemplated its sad inhabitants. The three birds in the cage ceased their agitated flight and, as if lost in a trance, they stood looking at me, their pupils riveted on this strange individual who, in turn, was watching them from outside the bars that confined them. They watched me and I watched them. In their eyes I saw a pain and a yearning, the desire for freedom, and the longing to fly again. I felt their distress and the brokenness in their souls; I felt, too, their nervous drive to escape from that prison.

Possessed by an overwhelming urge, I opened the cage and tore the door almost clear off. I took a step back, allowed my winged brothers to come forth, and, as if guided by an impulse, they flew in orderly fashion, one after another, through the door of the cage and then out the window toward boundless freedom.

My chest swelled with a joy that exploded inside me like an infinite blast when I saw that the birds were free. I went to the balcony and watched them fly away into the boundless sky.

Up above, the sun continued on its way, its rays now oblique, its enchanting light bouncing off the leaves of the camphors. I went back into the room, and for a moment I stood by the window, looking out. But the birds had already gone, so I sat down in the chair again and continued waiting. But this time the wait wasn't long. Once again, I heard something in the space to my right. They weren't murmurs this time, but voices intoning elaborate melodies and harmonies. The voices overlapped, their tones rising and then falling, some stopping and others starting, all together producing a sound that was strange and musical, but above all foreign and strange, or perhaps sinister and malicious. Once again I was full of curiosity. What was going on in this strange place? Who were the participants of this ceremony? What was the relationship between them and the person in the room across from me?

There was undoubtedly some link, because as soon as the chanting began in the one room, a heartbreaking and painful crying began in the other. I don't mean a light, meek sob, but the cry of a shattered soul, devastated with anguish and immersed in the deepest pain. I couldn't help but feel the heartbreak and bitter torment of this weeping creature in my own soul.

It was difficult for me to say with certainty how long all this lasted, but then it stopped, and the silence and tranquility prevailed once more. I was extremely confused and simultaneously impatient to know what was going on in those two rooms. My musings were interrupted by the sound of footsteps in the room across from me, and then by the sound of the knob as the door opened. Then I saw the shadow of a human silhouette and a woman coming through the door. I was awestruck to see that it was Fernanda Szabo, the girl I desired, the woman I knew and longed for. She stopped in front of her door and looked at me with an expression of surprise comparable to mine. She walked up and stood in front of me.

"I'm happy to see you" she said. "I felt very lonely in that room."

I understood these words with perfect clarity. I thought to myself that I would be very happy to stay with her in her room and alleviate her loneliness, and also that I would enjoy her company and her nearness, her bright eyes and her musical voice. These things I thought, as she stood in front of me, her hair fragrant, and her skin so soft. Then she came even closer and rested one of her gentle hands on my shoulder, brought her sensual lips closer to my ear and uttered a few words that I couldn't comprehend; I was so overwhelmed by her closeness and her touch, so entranced by the magic of feeling this woman next to me. I had never loved Fernanda, but I had desired her passionately. I had felt, or intuitively known, that the touch of her lips would have transported me to paradise. Then she uttered those words that I never did hear, intoxicated by her closeness and her touch; then she stood by my side, her lips close to my face, her hand on my shoulder, as if waiting for an answer, or a movement. I knew that I just had to turn my face in the direction of hers, and then my lips would find her mouth, her lips of flowers and honey. For a moment she seemed to hesitate and wait. I felt possessed by her touch and her smell, and thus passed an instant, or many moments, and then she turned slightly away. Her gentle hand slid from my shoulder to my elbow and then separated from my body. She took a step back and stopped, hesitated for a moment, and before returning to her room, she said to me: "I received a book from Gerardo. I was really surprised; I thought he had left or disappeared. But it's good ... the book, I mean ... it's good. Read it if you want. I left it on the shelf with the other books. Read it, it's good."

Fernanda said this about the book she received from Gerardo and then disappeared into her room. I was again overwhelmed by indescribable sensations, a fire from within and an unspeakable pain. But she was now far away, back in her room, and I was sitting in my chair again, wondering the meaning of the things that were happening around me.

Some more time passed. Everything was calm and quiet again. But the calm was interrupted by the noise of footsteps in the room to the right. Someone walked briskly to the door and closed it forcefully. I then realized that something was going to happen in that mysterious chamber. Almost immediately, the flame of the candle regained its brightness, this time with a magnificent shining light. I waited, cautiously and fearfully, because I knew that something was brewing in that room, but what it was, I couldn't imagine. Then it happened all at once. Without warning, a tremendous musical tone rang out in the silence, like the voice of a thousand torrents.

Perhaps it was a gong that uttered the sound and, just as unexpectedly, a tragic, shrill scream burst forth from the room across from me, an eerie wail, a voice torn with pain and supplication. But it lasted only a moment, for after a few seconds it was drowned out and lost, as the sound of the gong and the soft light of the candle in the room to the right also waned.

I looked out the window and discovered that the afternoon was growing dark, the sun was going away; twilight was growing, and the afternoon was dying. I got up and walked to the room in front of me, where Fernanda was, beautiful and distant. I reached the door, and on the threshold I stopped. Suddenly, like lightning, and with unexpected clarity, the words she uttered in my ears became clear as the morning light. She had said to me, "please save me." Then I entered the room where the woman I desired was, and I found her spread out on the floor, her whole body, voluptuous and sensual, scattered on the ground. In front of me, still growing and red, a pool of blood was turning into a small lake. The orange and pink light of the fading sun bounced off of it, producing iridescent flashes. My gaze traveled the length of the body of this splendid woman and found her throat opened from one side to the other, like a macabre smile.

With caution, yet no respect, the flies approached.

Honolulu, April 2017

A TWICE-TOLD TALE

Seduced by the aroma of coffee and the pleasant atmosphere of the place, I left the bustle of the avenues to sit down at one of the tables in this quiet refuge away from the whirlwind of the city. I took a few steps and looked around. Shiny floors with Arabesque tiles. Well-kept tables and walls covered with paintings, artistic images and portraits of writers. A lovely place.

Where might I sit? What would be the ideal spot for my morning reflections? Perhaps the corner featuring the portrait of Baudelaire?

Once again, I looked around, and my eyes naturally fell on a nearby table that had a book on it. I went over and grabbed it, looked around, and couldn›t find anyone who might be its owner or who demonstrated the slightest interest in the volume, the cover of which featured a strange, or at least singular and colorful image. So I approached the counter, and after ordering a coffee loaded with cream and chocolate, I asked the barista if he had any idea who the owner of the seemingly abandoned book might be. The barista looked at me with surprise for a moment, hesitated for a second, and then told me that no one had sat in that spot for a long time, and that he didn't know whose it could be. So I went back to the table, sat right down, took a sip of my delicious coffee, and picked up the book. I considered the possibility of incorporating it into my library if it happened to be of interest. So I turned to the table of contents and quickly read it. Then I leafed through the pages with the tips of my fingers, and among them I found a folded piece of paper. I opened it and read it with astonishment, and perhaps something approaching horror.

On the paper was written a short and terrible note. It said, "The old lady is dead. I killed her. The rotten old lady is dead."

For a moment I was taken aback by the shock of finding such a message, and I hardly noticed the fact that there was something curious and familiar about the handwriting of the note.

However, I gave the issue no more than a moment's consideration. I put the note back between the pages of the book and focused on savoring the delicious coffee in front of me and pondering the events that had occurred during the day.

Early in the morning I had visited the children's hospital, and Dr. Napoli had informed me, with a big smile and a dazzling sparkle in his eyes, that Reinaldo was fine, that the transfusion had been a complete success, and that my blood had saved his life. Naturally, my heart was flooded with joy. I didn't know Reinaldo, but I didn't need to know him to want to help him, to extend a saving hand by donating my blood so that he could live.

That's how my day started, with an immense joy that warmed my chest and made my heart glow. The meeting with Dr. Napoli was quite pleasant. He repeatedly offered me his thanks, and I told him that I would be at his disposal whenever he needed, that he could count on me at any time, and that it was an immense pleasure to be able to help in this way. So with a hug we said goodbye, and I started walking down the quiet tree-lined streets until I found the main avenues and the hustle and bustle of the city. Then I found this comfortable place, and now I was wondering how to continue on with my day.

I felt inspired, touched by a magic, or a divine music. I felt the presence of the muse and the verses came to me. Emotions piled up in my soul and rhymes in my voice; words hounded me, chased me, cornered me, and then I had to write, put into words this glory that overflowed in me. I grabbed the book, took the last sip of coffee, and went back out to the street. I walked aimlessly, lost and drunk on the beauty with which the flow of language assaulted me:

"Crimson skies keenly burning,
From the cradle, my greatest yearning
O crimson waters of the sea
Now a man, I can but love thee".

Yes. Poetry adored me as I adored her, and so came the verses that reflected the light that surrounded and passed through me. Yes, I'm happy. The sun is shining, shining brightly, shining inside of me. And in this state of mind, I kept moving along the sidewalks and receiving verses from heaven, and in that ecstasy, I walked many blocks, hardly noticing them, so seduced and stunned was I by the beauty of the language.

Finally, a sound from the earth broke the spell. The phone rang. I answered it immediately, and I heard a voice say:

"Hello, can I speak to Eduardo Gombrowicz?"

"You certainly can. You're speaking to him right now. How can I help you?"

"Hi Eduardo. It's Lautaro. I was calling to thank you for your monthly contribution toward the neutering and feeding of the dogs at the shelter. Your help is very important for them, and I didn't want to miss the opportunity to thank you."

"Well Lautaro, thank you very much, but you don't have to call me every month to thank me. It's an absolute pleasure, and you have my gratitude for everything you do for the dogs, which is honorable work that is worthy of praise. I wish I could do something for them in a more direct way, like you do, stopping at nothing to help them. All right, Lautaro. I wish you all the best, and let's stay in touch. Anything you need, all you have to do is ask, and I'll be happy to help."

"All right, Eduardo. All the best to you as well. Talk to you soon."

"See you later."

And so the conversation ended, which gave me an idea for what my next step would be, and how I would move forward with my day. I decided to go to the market and buy some bird food. I bought a large, slightly heavy bag. I carried it to the park, and as I approached, the pigeons and sparrows began to fly towards me, surround me, and sing the songs of hungry birds.

They knew me, and we were friends. I wonder to what extent they understood that I loved them, that it gave me enormous pleasure to feed them, help them grow and reproduce and develop full and happy lives, and thus contribute to the health and prosperity of our beloved planet. I wasn't sure how much they understood, but when they flew around me and looked into my eyes, we all knew that there was a connection and a love between us, something enduring and divine.

So I spent the better part of the afternoon scattering the nutritious seeds on the ground and watching the birds eat. And in this pleasant activity I lingered until the bag was empty, but the birds' bellies were full, and the daylight slowly began to fade, and then I thought that the perfect way to conclude a day of pure delights would be to go to visit my mother. So after stopping at the store again to buy a hunk of Cambozola, I headed towards my mother's house, taking little bites of the delicious cheese.

The shadows were getting longer and the light was falling. The afternoon was expiring. I enjoyed the dying of the day as I enjoyed few things and, combined with a festival of dry leaves on the ground, which rustled with every one of my steps, such walks could be an enormous pleasure. So in this celebration of the senses, I walked to my mom's house, stopping to pick a rose from a garden to present to Teresa when I got there.

I finally arrived at the house and knocked on the door. After a moment I knocked again. But my mother made no attempt to open up, which surprised me. So I knocked one more time and waited, but nothing happened. I tried the doorknob, and I was surprised and alarmed to find that it turned. The door gave way and opened, so I took several steps inside and said: "Teresa...Mom. I have a flower for you," but she did not answer. It was seven forty-five in the evening, and the city was already a little dark and eerie. There was no way Mom would be out of the house. So I uttered her name once more, and the third time I shouted it, but there was no answer. I walked to the kitchen hoping to find her, but I didn't see her anywhere. Then I became alarmed. I thought I remembered something.

Suddenly I began to perspire, and my legs became weak. I ran clumsily to her room, and an instant before opening the door, I knew for certain that my mother was in there, because it would have been impossible for her to leave the room. Hesitantly, I pushed the door open and saw the bed from an angle. After taking three steps inside I saw one of her legs. I went further into the cheerless room, and I gradually began to make out the sight of my mother's whole body, and with a sensation like the breath of death itself, I realized that each of her limbs was separated from her body, and that her head was absent. Then a shiver of horror ran down my spine, and with a heavy resignation, I returned to the kitchen where I had left the book that

I had found that very morning in the café. I picked it up again and scrolled through the pages until I found the note, which I held once more in my hands, and I read.

It was then that I discovered what it was that had felt so near, so familiar about the script: it was the fact that the handwriting was none other than my own.

Honolulu, March 2018

ANNIVERSARY

I FOUND the letter announcing our wedding: "Julieta Genet and Hector Bowen joyously unite for all eternity," and the memory of our wedding brought tears to my eyes. Today is March 13th, the day of our anniversary. I spent all week looking forward to the day that we would celebrate with the greatest joy our love and union. Every detail had been carefully planned out. This day would be, above all, a tribute to Julieta, the woman of my dreams. Every detail had been thought out: in the morning, breakfast in bed, the room full of flowers. I made the arrangements myself. I combined the roses in such a way as to express my passion for her. The aroma of jasmines perfumed the air, and tulips adorned every corner.

Right at noon, when the sun would come flooding through the dining room window, lunch would be prepared. Her favorite dishes. I had spent all of the previous day preparing the sauces, making the dough for the pasta, and seasoning the vegetables. At this point, everything would be cooked to perfection, and the flavors would be combined in the most delicious medley for her. When she sat down at the table, she would see how much I adored her.

In the afternoon, she would receive a gift that would be the physical manifestation of the feelings that overflowed from my heart and flooded my chest. An item created by my hands so that she would know she was a shining light from heaven. Every moment of the day had been carefully planned in her honor to express my total devotion and commitment to our union.

Only one thing remained for it to be the perfect afternoon. I had to go to the patisserie to buy her chocolates to enjoy with her tea. I stepped out of the apartment into the sunlight, completely satisfied that the day was going to plan, walked happily to the patisserie and bought an assortment of chocolates, put them in the loveliest box, and made my way back to the apartment.

When I entered the dining room, I found Julieta dismembered and scattered about the room. The colors of her insides decorated the floor and the walls. Small portions of her body were strewn about every corner of the room. I knew it was Julieta because her head was still intact on the table, like the perfect ornament.

I fled the room, seized by the deepest desperation. What inconceivable madness had taken place there? I couldn't imagine, but I felt as though I had been blinded by a pain that knows no parallel in the annals of human suffering, stifled by an unfathomable grief. I was destroyed, crushed by a pain beyond explanation.

I felt only this, and the absence of my beloved wife who fed every living cell of my body like the oxygen I breathe; more essential than that oxygen, since without that I could die in seconds, but without her I could live in eternal suffering.

Possessed by these emotions, I went out into the street and walked directionless among indifferent crowds and down dark alleys. What happened then, I only vaguely recall as a hazy memory. The searing pain of my lost love smothered it all like a dreadful blanket. Things that I can scarcely recollect took place: I went into bars, spoke incoherent words, I cried the most bitter tears a man can cry, I crawled down dirty streets and then I fell into darkness.

When I opened my eyes, I found that the black moon was watching me with an icy heartlessness. I turned my head and it hit a hard surface. I lost consciousness again, or perhaps I slept. In my dream, I visited the most desolate regions and the darkest places that the human soul might witness. I saw torrents of blood, a flood of horrors, dead things that befoul the souls of men. I felt the dread of Julieta's absence, her radiant smile that I would never see again, her heavenly touch now beyond possibility. I was broken and overcome by this macabre reality that I refused to believe, and thus transpired the hours of what seemed an endless night. When I awoke, the night was still dismally dark, and the black moon continued its indolent vigil.

Guided by impulse, I picked up the abandoned pages of the day's paper. The headlines announced the victories of a renowned tennis player. The publication date was March 17th. I didn't remember seeing the light of day recently. Nor had I felt hunger or thirst, seemingly. I only felt, in my whole being, the want of my lost love, the woman for whom my heart beat—sensual and destroyed, without whom my life could be no more than a desolate place of shadows.

It was then that I noticed for the first time that I wasn't alone. In front of me, lying on the ground and resting his chin on his hands, a homeless man was watching me. He looked dirty and downtrodden. His long, tangled hair no doubt housed a multitude of insects. His face represented that which is darkest and most perverse of the human condition, and his stench was insufferable. Nevertheless, there was something highly odd about this man. His eyes held a strange flicker, a sign of intelligence, a lucid sobriety that contradicted his general appearance.

How could there be such precise clarity, such powerful certainty in the glance of this foul wretch? For a moment

I marveled at his eyes, but then, suddenly, I became terrified, for in an instant they changed. Perhaps they grew larger or smaller, or it was the intensity of his glance that I found so disconcerting. I wasn't sure what it had been, but something in those eyes had transformed and struck me with true fear.

I looked away and tried to get to my feet. I stumbled and fell. For the first time I noticed the smell of the salt water and of the putrid things that float on its surface, and I realized I was in the port. I lifted my eyes to the sky again, imploring, begging for a balm or some consolation, and I found once more that the black moon—heartless, distant, indifferent—was watching me.

And then, the vagrant who was lying in filth on the ground caught my attention again and, with disgusted shock, I realized that he was next to me, inches away, and if I was overpowered by his being so nauseatingly close, the horrible expression of satisfaction and the disturbing smile sketched across his face made me feel all the more so.

I then came to the disconcerting realization that as close as this man was to me, I didn't even see him approach; I never noticed the slightest movement of his body. Then I cried out, or perhaps I laughed in terror. His hideous smile still disfigured his face, and this, combined with his bright, sagacious eyes, instilled in me a singular horror. What was this man smiling about? Why wouldn't he remove his gaze from me? Why couldn't I remove mine from his? Into what sunless abyss was my soul descending as I looked into those sinister black eyes?

Then a new terror came over me, for as I looked into them, they changed again, and though they maintained their perfidious expression, something in them, perhaps their shape or color, was different. And those perverse eyes, along with his odious smile, plunged me into a state of terror.

Shaken as I was, it was impossible for me to withstand the emotions that overpowered me. I felt that in those eyes there was an encrypted message, a code, something he wanted me to know, and I understood that this man had a purpose, that he was the bearer of dismal news. There was something I needed to know, but I couldn't imagine what it might be.

I stood up. I ran, or tried to run. I looked up again and found that the glimmering moon was no longer in the sky. In vain I searched imploringly in every celestial corner but, overcome with despair, I noticed that the terrible moon had abandoned me.

I felt the overwhelming urge to flee from the foul presence of that man. I needed to escape and get away from him, but when I looked around, I couldn't find him. He had completely vanished, like dew in the afternoon. How could it be possible? A moment before he was lying on the ground among the garbage, looking at me with his loathsome expression of both sorrow and pleasure.

I fell to my knees. I crawled. I tried to stand up. With great effort, I managed to walk along the docks, without direction or destination. The impossibility of controlling myself pressed down on me and made my head swim. My vision became an unstoppable whirlwind, and then I lost my balance.

I was racked by the guilt of an unspeakable crime that I couldn't quite recall.

I felt myself fall and hit the ground. I could feel the boards of the dock against my body. I found myself lying on them, seized by a scorching sensation. The boards of the dock seemed to burn like violent suns, and their very contact seared my skin.

I got up to escape the pain, but that did nothing to assuage the oppressive heat, the terrible fire that surrounded me. I then realized, to my terror, that the burning sensation wasn't coming from the boards of the dock, but from inside me. I felt the flames around my heart, burning ferociously in secret. I felt as though my whole body was enveloped in the embers of hell.

Honolulu, March 2017

THE BOOK IS REAL

GERARDO is dead. Nobody really knows what happened to him. He simply disappeared, but the circumstances suggest that this absence isn't just permanent, but that there is something tragic in it. Maybe something sinister. Definitely something murky.

His behavior in the weeks leading up to his disappearance all of us found curious, but some of us read it as the sign of a change in our friend's personality. Well, I wasn't particularly close to him, but we belonged to the same group and frequented the same places, the same bars and cafés.

It is hardly surprising that a romantic altercation set up a rivalry of sorts between us, though I never bore him any ill will; I had after all been the victor in that particular contest and Silvana chose me. However, Gerardo had clearly developed a dislike for my person, that much was clear to me. So I preferred to keep things polite, keep my distance and never had any interaction with him without the company of some mutual friend. So little did I see of him that the mutation in his personality was to me clearer and more apparent. The boy was changing, there was not the least doubt, and it was not a change for the better, that much we could all see: his eyes had darkened, his gaze was opaque and evasive: it never met the eyes of the people he was speaking to, and his conversation was fragmented and disjointed, as if his mind were wandering from place to place but always buzzing around certain topics, certain themes he found interesting or maybe was obsessed by, and of such matters he would speak incessantly while gesticulating wildly and pulling faces, his stare lost in the ground or the sky.

On those occasions, we would sideline him, but he would just keep on talking to himself, staring at the ground and making strange gestures. He had changed greatly, that much was clear to all, even physically: he was thinner than ever, his cheekbones jutting, his skin cracked and dry; his hair had lost its shine and was graying; his skin was pocked with sores and his clothes with bloodstains.

What had happened to this fellow was a mystery to everyone. These changes wrought themselves out of nothing, and then, a few weeks later, he disappeared, vanished completely, without trace or explanation or signs of any kind to provide us with a clue as to what had become of him. So we looked for him, waited for him, posted his photo in all kinds of media and broadcast it far and wide. Nothing was of any use, all our efforts were in vain; we never heard of him again or found out what had happened to him. So, after several months, when our efforts finally ran aground along with our hopes, when we privately and ultimately realized Gerardo had gone for good, we decided to hold a sendoff-cum-funeral for him, a ceremony to bid him goodbye and let him go.

It was short and emotional. The sorrow was tangible as the autumn leaves that carpeted the ground, as the fresh air on our faces, and the black clouds looming in the sky seemed to chime with our mood of sadness and nostalgia. In some indubitable way, the firmament knew that we had lost someone and that our hearts ached.

As I said, the ceremony was brief, and when it had finished, Gerardo's mother asked, through inconsolable tears, if anyone would be willing to visit her son's apartment to tidy and pack his belongings; she found the prospect of setting foot in there quite impossible, but it had to be cleared. Maybe because I felt beholden to him, maybe because I wanted, in vain, to make amends to him for not being Silvana's chosen one, I offered to do the job and to do it in the friendliest, most respectful way I could as a final tribute to Gerardo.

I was given the key by his mother, and as soon as my duties allowed, I set off for the apartment to start on the job of cleaning and tidying. The days leading up had been warm and sunny, the birds seemed to revel in the glories of the day with their winged music, and the sunlight filtering through the branches of the trees was a riot, a celebration of fantastic things that seemed to float in the air. So I found it quite remarkable that the day I chose to start cleaning Gerardo's apartment the sky was black as the grave, the air as cold as the Arctic, and I could find no birds to dispel with their songs the heavy gloom entombing everything around me.

I thought about leaving the cleaning for another day. I got sidetracked and delayed. It struck me that a cold day was an invitation to visit the movie theater. Yes! Sure! Going to the movies was a great idea: any movie would be better than walking these dismal streets that felt like they held a premonition heralding something strange and sordid or morbid and out of place. In short, with utter clarity, it dawned on me that I would rather do anything but visit the gloomy abode of this funereal figure. But I had made his mother a promise, and now I was tarred with the obligation to keep it. So, heavy with dismay, I trudged off, taking one step after another as if my feet weighed tons. A voice in my conscious mind kept telling me to stop, or change course, or do something else. But, as I said, I had made a promise, and it was up to me to keep it. So I reached the apartment and took out the key. But before I could fit it in the lock, it slipped through my fingers and fell in the mud.

I picked it up, wiped away the sticky sludge, and finally managed to open the door. As I entered the apartment, an icy shiver ran through my body. I was overwhelmed by an immediate sluggishness of the spirit the moment I crossed the threshold, and somehow I knew dark things were massing on the horizon. But I paid them no mind; I was on a mission and had set out to complete it as efficiently as possible. So I decided to ignore all these pointless superstitions and carry out my purpose as swiftly as possible in order to get the whole matter over and done with.

The place was dark, and a pall of sorrow lay over every object. Tangible, it spread through the air and into my lungs. I could breathe this harrowing sorrow, this darkness looming over everything. I took a few steps and looked around. The curtains were drawn across the windows, and the chaos in the apartment's two rooms was everywhere. Cleanliness was clearly not a habit Gerardo had adopted, nor tidiness. There were books on the dining-room table and the bedroom floor, some caked in dust, others with pages torn out; there were vinyl records scattered around the room and a broken turntable; there was a box full of packages; there were dirty dishes and rotted food in the kitchen. The place was total chaos, and I guessed it would take at least two or three full days to make it somewhere pleasant and presentable, somewhere habitable; at the moment, it looked like the cave of an animal.

Before embarking on my labors, I sat down in a dust-laden chair and took a look around me. A painting depicting a sordid scene hung on the wall: two men looked on with sinister smiles while a third devoured the entrails of a child lying on the ground. I pondered how twisted someone who hung a similar image on his dining-room wall must be, and then, in utter astonishment, I realized that equally hideous images decorated the other walls of the dining room, and the bedroom as well.

It struck me that the macabre realm of Gerardo's home in fact exactly reflected the person he had become: a morbid, wraithlike creature.

I got to my feet, went to a window and drew back the curtain, but all that came through the window was the shadows of a dead tree. I decided it was impossible to improve the atmosphere or energy of the place, so I chose to get down to the task in hand right away and finish up as soon as possible. But where to start? I looked around again. This time my eyes lighted upon another of the bizarre decorative scenes hanging on the walls. It showed the moment of a burial, with all the mourners grinning eagerly under the shade of an ancient oak.

To one side of the painting was a shelf of books and journals. A natural urge led me to the shelf, where I pulled out one of the journals and, after examining the first few pages, I found that it was handwritten and that each entry was dated.

I was suddenly engulfed by an unusual emotion when I realized that I had come across what appeared to be Gerardo's personal journal and that it might contain a key to understanding his abrupt transformation and disappearance. So, I sat down again in one of the filthy chairs and began to read:

"The book is real. It truly exists. It isn't some madcap belief or superstition; it is an incontrovertible reality. I have the ultimate proof: I have found it! I found the book and have a copy in my possession.

"The stories say that it is an evil book, that it has the power to derange those who read it and to poison their souls. This is hard to believe, I know. But I have read a lot of stories that tell of such things. People read the book and then begin to change,

they become unhinged and start doing weird things, things normal people wouldn't do. Sometimes the change is gradual and people change slowly, but from what I had read, other times the change can be sudden and people who have read the book become degenerates, so to speak, or something like that, and start doing mischief to themselves and others. Now I have a copy of the book here with me, and I ask myself if everything I've read about it is true. There is only one way to find out then: I have to read the book and see what happens, see whether something happens to me or whether there's nothing to it. It would be like an experiment: I don't know if I'll turn into a nasty piece of work or monster or what, but I'm still excited and can't wait to read it to see what happens.

"The strange thing is I believe in the book. I mean, I believe the things I've read about the book and that it has the power to ruin people and make them evil. But I don't care, I still can't wait to read it. It'll be weird, but I've found a copy of the book and know I'm going to read it.

"Apparently, people go crazy or get kind of wild and start doing weird things. I read that some flagellate themselves, that others torture their children and things like that, and it all begins when they read the book. It still isn't clear to me what it is about the book or how it transmits its poison to those who read it. I have no idea how something like that can happen, but it only makes me want to read it more. So I'm going to start it tonight. For now, I'll just enjoy having it. I have been reading about this book for so many years, and I never thought I would ever find it."

This entry was dated nine weeks earlier and, with a shudder, I recalled that it was around then that Gerardo began to alter his habits and transform his behavior. However, I dismissed this as mere coincidence and gave no credit to the nonsense I had just read in Gerardo's journal. An evil book? With the power to adversely affect its readers and alter their behavior? Could there be a more ridiculous notion? No doubt these outlandish writings would be just another manifestation of this fellow's troubled state of mind.

I put the journal back on the shelf where I had found it, determined to get down to cleaning and tidying at once. However, much of the afternoon had by now been consumed between one thing and another, and with it my desire to devote myself to the work, so I dithered about how to proceed. But then a sense of obligation prompted me to get to my feet and down to the task in hand.

I began with the kitchen to get rid of the stench, which invaded the whole apartment. I cleaned up all the garbage that had piled up in the sink, and I emptied the fridge. I washed the dishes and tidied them away. The cupboard above the sink was filled with moldering condiments and a few cans of non-perishable food. I threw away the condiments, cleaned the shelves and opened the cans of food. Then I took them outside and emptied them on the lawn for the wild animals to eat. As I looked up, I noticed the sky was beginning to darken. The sun had already sunk, and the wind was heaving black clouds over the horizon.

I felt rather disappointed at how unproductive the day had been but decided that I would come back tomorrow for a little longer and with more focus, and make up for what I hadn't done today. So I picked up my backpack, closed the door, turned the key and started walking home. Next to the path leading to the sidewalk, where I had emptied the foodcans, some cardinals were pecking at the food, while a squirrel studied it carefully and sniffed the air. The scene made me smile, and I set off with a warm feeling inside me. Then I remembered that poor broken man Gerardo and his damned book, and the warmth quickly faded.

The next day I was up early. I ate a quick breakfast and set out for the apartment, determined to move forward with cleaning as far as I possibly could. It was another cold, dark, foggy morning. The atmosphere around me felt weirdly like a reflection of my own mood: inexplicably, the moment I had set about cleaning that apartment, I had felt as dark and foggy as the morning.

I couldn't stop thinking about the book and Gerardo's obsession with it, and, as I set foot in the apartment, I immediately went to the shelf with the journals on and started reading them:

"Finding the book was just a matter of luck. Well, I thought it was luck at first, but now I think it was fate. This had to be. Either that, or the book wanted me to find it. I must have thought so much about this book, read so much about it, wanted so much to have it that, in the end, it decided to seek me out. The book must have wanted me to find it. That must be it. It felt to me like a coincidence, but I don't believe in coincidences, so it must have been fate.

"As it happened, I was in church. I don't believe in the church or any of its lies, but the parish priest needed some removing rubble from the church garden and had hired me to do the work. But then the guy asked me to wait while he had a word with some woman, this skinny, bony broad dressed in black with pale, scaly skin.

"The woman told the priest that she had a copy of the book he was looking for and that she could give it to him in return for a favor. The priest told her he would pay any sum for the book, that he had a whole month's donations from the congregation at his disposal, and that she could have them all. The woman told him she didn't want money, she wanted something else, but I couldn't hear what it was because the broad whispered it in the priest's ear.

"Then the priest laughed and, almost shouting, replied, 'Sure, no problem, whatever you want, whatever you want, lady! But where's the book? Do you have it with you?'

"I have it here in my purse," she said.

"Then there was this terrible noise in the room adjoining the one where the priest and the skinny lady were talking, and they went to see what was happening. I had been watching everything through the curtain that separated the rooms. I saw the two of them go into the other room. But the woman left her purse behind on the chair, and, as if guided by some force, I went right in without stopping to think, grabbed it and rushed out. I paused at the pews in front of the altar, opened up the purse and looked inside. Without a second thought, I grabbed the book, tossed aside the purse and ran out of church.

"When I think about it, I can find no explanation. I don't know why I did it. I had no idea which book they were talking about, and I had no reason to think it was the same book I had been searching for. I acted on impulse, without thinking, guided by an urge, but everything turned out well. I'm back home now, and I have this book that I wanted so much and that I searched so long for."

So Gerardo stole the book. For some reason, it didn't surprise me. I barely knew the guy, but being a thief fit really well with the opinion I held of him.

I laid the journal down on the table for a moment and looked around. The apartment was still a mess, but once again I found myself spending my time reading instead of working.

So I stood up and went to the shelf where the books were. I opened one of the boxes I had brought with me and stowed them in it, along with some framed photographs on the same shelf and a few other objects lying around.

That was when my eyes alit on a box on the floor, to one side of the dining-room table. It was open and contained several neatly wrapped packages. I grabbed them and found that they were all ready to be mailed, with names and addresses written on them. They were all the same size and clearly contained exactly the same object to be sent to all five people. Gerardo apparently had had no time to take them to the post office, so I thought it would be a noble gesture to run the errand for him.

I checked the packages and read the names and addresses: Hector Bowen in Turdera; Ricardo Havel inTemperley; Eduardo Gombrowicz in Turdera; Fernanda Szabo in Adrogué. The last package held an uncomfortable surprise for me. It was addressed to Silvana. My Silvana. My girlfriend.

I stopped dead in my tracks, clutching the package. I thought about opening it. Some inner voice or instinct drove me to destroy it or toss it into the garbage—to do anything with it other than send it.

I put the packages back in the box and began to pace the room. On the one hand, I was overcome by a sense of obligation to this fellow; I think I always felt I owed him, maybe I wanted to make it up to him for being the victor in our contest over Silvana's heart. On the other hand, a powerful voice inside me urged me to leave these packages alone or destroy them. They stirred dark feelings in me, but I fought off such fateful thoughts, put the packages on one side and went back to my cleaning.

Eventually the afternoon dwindled and, as the sun drew toward the horizon, I felt I had worked hard enough and could carry on the following day. I looked around and saw the apartment looking considerably tidier and cleaner, though there was still a little more work ahead, maybe a couple of days.

I locked the door behind me and set off. The sun was setting, and the streets were as gray as the pallid light of the sky. The memory of the packages I had found in the box and my doubts as to what to do with them came back to haunt me. But I was tired and didn't want to devote my energy to the issue, so I put it aside for now and plodded on toward home, gripped by an overpowering sense of unease.

Next morning I awoke with the image of the packages playing in my mind and the whole question of the evil book spinning around my head. I felt myself possessed by a foggy, troubled mood. Clearly something was adversely affecting my state of mind, but I found it impossible to say what.

I resolved to go back to the apartment and finish the cleaning as soon as possible so I could close this whole chapter. But no sooner had I arrived at the apartment than I was seized by the urge to explore the shelf of Gerardo's journals further and go on reading about this book he had stolen from a holy man, a man of God.

I spent several hours reading and finished two of the journals. The first dealt with the history of this so-called accursed book and the fact that there seem to exist different versions of the book, or different books, with the power to subtly or violently poison the souls of those who read it. From this journal, I copied a few paragraphs:

"The book has long existed. It has existed as long as men have, but, through the ages, it has taken different forms in different cultures and in different languages. Yet, in essence, it is the same: a book that bears within it a poison, a spiritual venom. And, once the book is read, its reader is impregnated with that poison, and it remains in them forever.

"Readers become perverted and altered by the poison. They change their behavior and sometimes change physically as well. They put themselves at the book's disposal, as if they were its

servants, and then devote themselves to doing evil in one way or another.

"I realize many people might not believe that this is true, that such a book exists. But they are wrong, because there is indeed a version of just such a book which has been circulating for thousands of years, a subtle version whose poison is almost imperceptible but is very real and very destructive. It enters people's souls unbeknown to them: they are unaware they are reading an evil book meant to pervert them; instead, they believe they are reading a book like any other. It leaves its poison without them realizing, and these people do the book's bidding and make it part of their lives, and so pass the book and the poison on to others."

The second journal was very different in tone. It dealt not with the book or its history or its different versions, but showed how drastic the change being wrought in Gerardo was.

I discovered that the transformation in the fellow's personality and physiognomy was also expressed in his writings. I copied out a few passages that most forcefully caught my attention:

"Whether or not I am the same man, I do not know. I feel different. I feel very different. I have read one of the book's stories and, since I did, something has happened, something bad. I can no longer sleep, but I dream constantly, and my dreams are black; they are nightmares, dark and horrible. It all began with that story I read, which left something in me, like some evil seed now growing inside me."

"I know it was that story that damaged me. I could feel it as soon as I read it; I felt that with every word I read, it was injecting something wicked into my body, and now it feels like the poison's inside of me and I don't know how to get it out."

"I cannot resist the urge to keep reading. I know it is damaging me, I know it is poisoning me, but I cannot stop reading. The book talks to me, the book wants me to read it, as if it were a living thing calling to me, speaking to me, and I know I sink deeper at every sitting, yet I cannot stop reading. I know the harm it does me, yet I keep reading."

"I think about those who have hurt me, they are always in my mind. I used to forgive them, but now I think about them all the time and don't want to forgive them anymore. No. Now I want to kill them. Or, better still, torture them, make them suffer. The idea came to me when I read another of the stories in the book, and it spread through my head like a virus, a virus I now have all through my body. So I only think about doing them harm, paying them back for what they did to me, but paying them back double, more than double, because I am not a fair guy; no, now I am a man of the book, I work for the book, I do the book's bidding, and it bids me to make them suffer, to destroy them utterly."

"The book is in my head all the time. When I read it, it feels like it's alive, like it's speaking to me as a person, I feel like I'm at its service, like I've become the book's instrument, and the book wants to wreak evil."

"When I look in the mirror, I see a strange new face and am tortured by the feeling that I am lost forever. I feel different inside, as if my blood is different, or something is different, and I don't like it. My hatred for the man I am now has assumed giant proportions. My thoughts are always bleak and nightmarish, and my eyes too have turned dark, as have my ideas. The whole world seems to have turned dark."

"I have a plan. I know how to torture them, I know how to repay them for the harm they have done me. These filthy people will pay for it, I shall make them pay, they will pay for it with pain."

"I can scarcely believe the power the book has over me. After reading it several times, I have reread it again and feel as if I am falling into an ever-deepening well."

"The grim images I see in my mind are becoming darker, and I never see the light anymore."

"I hate them, I hate them and I shall destroy them utterly."

"Perhaps this will be my last entry. My mind is in utter confusion, I seldom think clearly or logically. I feel plunged into delirium."

"I have a feeling that something is happening, something terrible. I hear a voice that speaks of doing harm, not only to others but also to myself. It is the voice of one of the characters in the book. I know I shall destroy myself, be the scourge of myself, and that my soul is already lost. And now I have a plan not only to destroy those who hurt me, but to destroy myself. I have a plan and I am going to put it into action."

Once again I spent a large part of the afternoon reading Gerardo's journals instead of working. The reading caught me in its web, I have to admit. I could hardly believe the lunatic ravings this fellow had fallen into. I couldn't believe anyone could lose their sanity so fast or so sweepingly, but by now it was clear to me that Gerardo had gone quite mad. My mind could not cope with the amount of nonsense he was willing to believe, and I suddenly felt a profound sadness for him.

I looked around me and my heart sank to discover that there was still much work to be done, so I leaped into action, focused my energies and, without further distractions, threw myself into work.

By the end of the afternoon, the apartment was spick and span, and I was brimming with satisfaction at a job well done. The kitchen was spotlessly clean and full of the scent of flowers, the bedroom perfectly tidy, as was the living room. Gerardo's few belongings were packed away in two boxes for his mother to pick up, and all I had to figure out was what to do with the packages for the mail. I was tired and didn't feel like thinking about it. I picked up the box containing the parcels and decided that the right thing, the honorable thing, would be to take them to the post office and mail them to their addressees, so I carried it to the door.

But when I got there, I remembered that there was only one of Gerardo's journals left to read. So I went back to the shelf, grabbed the volume in question, put it in the box along with the parcels and left the apartment.

The first thing I did the next day was go to the post office and mail every one of the packages, except the one addressed to Silvana. I didn't want to think about it anymore and paid little heed to the inner voice warning me not to mail them. I reasoned that mailing them was the right thing to do. I felt it was the least I could do for this poor fellow, so I walked to the post office, dispatched the packages, and put the whole thing behind me. Then I set off for Silvana's house.

The morning was as dark, gloomy, foggy and cold as the previous ones had been. The gray of the streets was a reflection of the sky above and a perfect expression of the atmosphere of utter dejection that loomed over the city. I trudged along, slowly, wearily, as if some mighty force were trying to drag me back or stop me dead. I thought of taking in a movie to lighten my mood, to try and leave behind this overwhelming dejection, this inescapable feeling that something was wrong or out of place. Or maybe it was some premonition heralding something terrible. Either way, I was overtaken by a gloom I could not throw off and the cause of which I could not identify. But there was nothing of any interest showing at the movies, so I decided not to waste my time.

I trudged on down the bleak streets toward Silvana's house but couldn't resist the urge to take a detour to a café on main street. I ordered a pot of tea and a slice of peach pie, and sat looking out at the street. And as I watched the ragged crowds through the windows, I asked myself what might be the reason for this weariness and malaise I was feeling. I turned the matter over and over in my mind, trying to reason it through, but I could find no explanation.

Everything seemed to be good. I had fulfilled my obligation to Gerardo's mother, I had done the right thing by mailing the packages and carrying out his wish for the recipients to receive their gifts, or whatever the packages were. I had a beautiful fiancée I adored, and generally my life was running perfectly. I couldn't think of anything that was out of place. Yet I couldn't shake off this intolerable feeling of disquiet, as if something terrible was about to happen that I couldn't put my finger on.

Lost in thought as I was, much of the morning slipped by, and, when I had finished my tea and all that was left of the pie were the crumbs, I stood up and left the place to rejoin the crowds on the street.

I had walked maybe twenty or thirty yards when I heard a voice behind me shouting:

"Sir. You forgot something."

I turned around and saw the waiter from the bar approaching with the parcel for Silvana in his hands.

"This is yours, Sir. You left it on the table,' he said to me, stretching out his hand holding the parcel.

"Thank you very much," I said. I took it and carried on walking.

I eventually reached Silvana's house without having managed to shrug off the heaviness and disquiet I felt or understanding what was causing it. Her sister told me she was out but that she would be back soon. I said I had a package for her and asked if she could give it to Silvana as soon as she got back. I fished it out of my backpack but, as I was about to hand it to her, my grip slackened and the package fell to the floor. A strange voice in my mind urged me not to pick it up, to leave it where it lay, yet I crouched down, picked it up and handed it to Silvana's sister.

I said goodbye and trudged off down the pavement, feeling even more uneasy than I had before. By the time I reached home, I felt devastated, harrowed and without the smallest spark of energy. But, as I lay back on my bed, I remembered the last volume of Gerardo's journal I had brought back with me but had not yet read. I fetched it and lay down again. When I opened it, a loose page fell on my stomach.

It seemed to be a letter, undated and lacking the recipient's name. This is what it said:

"You'll pay for this, you dirty bitch.

"Do you really believe that piece of filth is better than me? Do you really think he can love you more than I do, better than I do? What were you thinking of when you cast my love aside for that of a piece of trash who will never love you the way I do or worship you with the passion I do or idolize you as I do?

"Yet you chose him, didn't you. And you treated me as if I was worth nothing and spurned all my love and everything I offered you as if it were worth nothing, and I gave you my heart and you trampled it underfoot like so much garbage. I gave you my heart, and you trampled all over it. I gave you the most valuable thing I had, I gave you my soul and you didn't care, it was worth nothing to you, as if everything I am and everything I offered you were nothing and worth nothing.

And all for what? For that worthless worm who isn't worth a quarter what I am, who isn't even worth the garbage stuck to the soles of my shoes.

"How could you have chosen him? I am far more of a man than him: I am braver than him, stronger than him, smarter

than him, I am in every way better than him. Yet you didn't choose me, you chose him, and now you'll pay, you bitch, you'll pay for tossing me aside for a worm who is worth nothing and for trampling all over me and treating me as if I were nothing.

"I have a little present ready for you. I'm sending it to you, bitch, and when you open it and read it, you'll get what's coming to you, your own little piece of hell. I already know, I've been through it, and I also know you will never escape, your soul will rot and burn, it will burn like souls burn in hell, it is what you deserve, you filthy bitch, it is what you deserve for trampling on my heart.

"You will pay, you wretched woman, I swear you will, because the gift I have for you comes disguised as something harmless, but it is not; it is a poison that will burn you like fire, but you won't know until it's too late, and, by the time you realize, there won't be anything you can do to stop it, you'll be contaminated, forever, because the poison gets inside you from the first page you read, and it stays there forever, till you burn, till you rot."

My reading of this disturbing page was interrupted by the sound of my cellphone. I picked it up and read the message. It was from Silvana and it said: "Hello, my love. I got the package you left me. Thanks so much for bringing it in personally. It's a book. I read the first story, and I liked it. I really liked the cover, too. It's eye-catching: such an unusual, colorful image. Come by the house later, and we'll have dinner together."

I felt utterly confused. My mind couldn't order all these things. I picked up Gerardo's letter again and went on reading.

"It strikes me as only fair that my enemies should pay for the things they have done to me, and you are my enemy, you

dirty bitch. You all have to pay. I used to want to forgive them, now I want to make them suffer. I owe it to the book. I can feel it, I can feel its influence, and I feel like it's using me, and now it's my turn to hurt, and I shall hurt you all and make you all pay for your offenses, for the things you have all done to me.

"*My idea is a simple one. I found the book, or the book found me, and now I know that its poison is powerful and that there is no escaping it. I also know I am doomed and my lucidity is waning and my despair is growing all the time. I am falling deeper and deeper into despair, because there is no escape. I have to make the most of the time I have left. I don't know how much time I have left. I have to make the most of it. I've already made copies of the book. I'm running out of time, and I have to make the most of it. I have already made copies of the book, now I have to send them to them. I'll send them the copies and pass on the poison. I've already made the copies and had them bound, now I have to send them out. I've made the copies and had them bound, and they look great, so I wrapped the parcels and wrote on each the name of my enemies, the sons and daughters of a damned mother, and they will pay for it, they will pay for the things they have done to me, and I shall send them the book and pass on the poison to them, I have already wrapped the packages and written their addresses on them and written their names on them, and I am going to make them pay. I shall send them the book and pass on the poison, and they shall pay, but I have little time.*"

Honolulu, November 2018

CIRCLES AROUND THE MOON

ILAID my head back on the pillow intending to continue with my reading. I found the most comfortable position and picked up the book again. With any luck, the irritating noises would be through and I'd be able to finish reading *The Circular Ruins,* which I was finding fascinating. I couldn't wait to find out what would come of the main character's bizarre dreams, so I opened the book and began to read, but two or three pages in, the noises started again, only this time it was an argument between a man and a woman that was taking place on the other side of the door. But that wasn't my business. I just wanted to be left in peace to finish the story, so I tuned them out and tried to concentrate on reading.

I read another page, and then the voices and the noises started up again. It seemed the argument was getting worse, because the voices at times turned to shouting, and the banging, at first distant and faint, became more intense.

I wondered what the banging could be, and during another pause from my reading, they became louder and drew nearer, and my irritation at the distraction gave way to worry. Nevertheless, I tried to brush the issue aside and reimmerse myself in the story. I got comfortable in bed again and tried to read, when I heard a shout from outside the door. It was the stifled voice of a woman, which left me stunned for a moment, followed by the raging bellowing of a hoarse voice. It was impossible to keep reading. I put down the book and sat still, listening from my bed, but there was complete silence. I could hear nothing but the movement of the curtains as they moved in the wind. It seemed I might be able to get back to reading and finally finish the story, when the voices returned, but now they were a confusion of violent shouting. The man's voice sounded like an earthquake, and the woman's voice was a horrible shriek, a terrified plea. Whatever it was that was happening in the next room, on the other side of that door, was turning into something truly alarming.

I've never been a busybody, and I think people should sort out their own problems, but I was beginning to wonder if some tragedy was about to take place and if I could do something to prevent it.

Then the noises resumed, but this time they were louder and stronger. With every crash, the floor and walls vibrated, as the woman's voice turned to a muffled high-pitched moan. This alarmed me. Something serious was definitely happening. I got up. As I hesitated, and the seconds passed, the shouts sounded closer than ever, more piercing and tortured. I heard rapid steps crossing the adjacent room and a terrific bang against the wall dividing our rooms. The man's voice sounded like thunder in the sky, and the woman's was a desperate cry, a scream for help.

I ran to the door and frantically pulled on the handle, which wouldn't turn, all the while the wall shook from the crashing, and the woman's voice was an anxious cry for help. Possessed by a mad panic, I grabbed the door handle and shook the door, banging on it, trying to knock it down, as a barrage of shrieking and begging exploded from the other side. The handle wouldn't give, the door wouldn't open, and the voice of the woman was growing weak and faint, it was dwindling and fading out. Then I charged against the door, shouting with all the power in my lungs "nooo..."

I found myself in bed, covered in sweat, awakened by the sound of my own voice, by that enraged yell escaping my throat.

For a moment I didn't know where I was, and it took me a few minutes to recover and understand that I was in my own room, and that everything that had transpired was no more than a dream—an incredibly vivid and intense one—but merely a dream. So I took a deep breath and sat in bed.

I turned on the bedside light and looked around, relieved to see that I was, in fact, in my room, and that everything was normal and fine. It was then that I heard the thumping in the next room for the first time, on the other side of the door, quiet at first, and the voices of the people seemed to be in conversation, but soon the thumps grew more intense, and the voices grew louder, in such a way that it seemed the conversation was starting to turn into an argument.

I was completely taken aback, still trying to wake up and comprehend what was happening, when the man's voice turned into a yell, and the woman's voice seemed to moan and beg. Completely stunned, I sat up, trying to organize my thoughts and figure out what was going on. I wondered if it was possible that the dream I had just had was a premonition, a warning, and that I was now presented with the opportunity to intervene in this episode and save the woman, or to help her, to do something.

So I jumped out of bed and, with the utmost urgency, put on my socks, my pants, and all my clothes. But just as I was dressed and ready to jump into action, I noticed the pervasive silence; only the sound of a butterfly trying to get through the window could be heard. I calmed myself down. I thought maybe my imagination was running away with me, that whatever was going on in the next room was normal and none of my business.

I waited a moment, and I was glad to see that there was nothing off or that deserved my attention. It was then that I heard a crash and a bang like something being repeatedly slammed against the wall, again and again, and the voices turned into shouts that became jumbled in my ears and confused in my mind. I ran desperately to the door. I grabbed the handle. I tried to turn it. Much to my anxiety, I found that, as I expected, it wouldn't turn. The door wouldn't open.

On the other side the storm grew worse. The shouts of the man tore at my ears. The woman's pleading stuck to me like tar. I had to act. I had to do something. But I couldn't. The door wouldn't open. The banging on the wall became more frequent and intense, the shouts deafening me, and the woman's begging, at first full-voiced and strong, began to fade and dissipate. I gathered momentum, filled my lungs with air, and with all my strength, I charged at the door, yelling from the bottom of my throat "nooo..."

The alarm went off. It was already four in the afternoon. Time to stop writing and focus on other activities required in life. I thought that someday perhaps literary glory would be mine, and then I could devote myself exclusively to writing. But for now I had to go to work, so I would finish the story another time. I sat in bed and started to put on my socks. It was then that I heard the banging and the voices in the next room. At first it seemed to be a man and a woman having a disagreement next door, but soon the voices were shouts and desperate pleading, as a thunderous noise like a volcano shook the building.

I immediately got up and ran to the door. The cries of the woman, at first full-voiced and strong, began to fade, as if they were trapped in her throat.

I desperately grabbed the door handle with all my strength. The shouts of the man filled the air, like a roar from the heavens. The handle wouldn't turn.

Honolulu, Hawaii, October 2018

A SUMPTUOUS FEAST

I NOW know that I'm a prisoner. I wish I knew where I was and how I got to this place, but all I can remember is a confused fog that blinds and surrounds me. There is a powerful throbbing, a sharp pain in my head, and then I remember being hit. The scenes come rushing like a wave back to my mind: the dark street, the cold air, the wait, the incessant lingering. Then the blow to the back of my head, the urgent voices; I remember falling on the wet sidewalk, the footsteps around me, my body being dragged, the suspension of consciousness. Now I wake up in this room, but where? Where am I?

I look around to discover that I'm in total darkness. All I can see is black, and my discouragement turns into an anxiety, one that I cannot allow to take me over. With the utmost effort, I manage to get a hold of my mind, stay calm, and rationalize the issue. I don't know where I am or how I got here, but the important thing is to figure out how to get out of this place. So I try to sit down, but as soon as I go to stand up straight against this hard, cold surface, I feel my head hitting the ceiling and the painful, needling torture again.

There is little space above me, which is disturbing, but I try not to despair. I must keep exploring this place; I decide to move to the right, and I crawl like a worm, like a reptile, and yet I'm not able to get very far. The wall is just a few inches away. I slide to the opposite side, and an icy dread comes over me. I discover that it's impossible to move in that direction either and that the enclosure in which I find myself is barely larger than a sarcophagus.

I try to remain calm, but it's hard not to succumb to hopelessness. I wonder if I have been buried alive, thrown into a plain coffin nailed shut, and cast into the deep, or if I am the victim of a macabre experiment, or a diabolical game. I wonder if it's a dream, a dark and horrible nightmare, but the stabbing pain in my head alerts me to the cruel reality in which I find myself. Then I notice something that I surprisingly did not discover until this moment: I am gagged, and my hands and my feet are bound. I'm locked in a tiny cold room, barely able to move, my limbs tied, without the slightest idea of what sinister plan may be unfolding around me. Then a desperate scream catches in my throat and bursts in my lungs.

***

«Gentlemen, it is an absolute pleasure to welcome you once again to my humble abode on the occasion of our monthly meeting,» said the legislator serenely, with a glowing expression on his face.

"Humble abode?" echoed the industrialist. "But your house is a palace. I can't even imagine what you do with so many rooms."

"Not to worry," replied the legislator. Believe me, we put the rooms to good use, and we're constantly imagining new ideas for how to use them."

Everyone laughed.

"In fact," continued the legislator, "later, after dinner, each of us will go to his respective room where he will find a delicious dessert to enjoy."

Everyone laughed again.

"I'm looking forward to it," commented the governor. "You always amaze us with your wit and your sense of fun and amusement."

"Of course, gentlemen, but that will be later. Now we are going to enjoy a tasty cigar and a glass of cognac," continued the legislator as the servants entered the room with snifters, bottles, and cigars. At that moment, the heavy ebony door opened wide to make way for one more member of the gathering.

"If it isn't our favorite agricultural tycoon!" exclaimed the governor enthusiastically. "Please come in. For a moment we thought we wouldn't be graced with your presence this evening."

"Of course you will!" replied the tycoon. "I wouldn't miss it for a thing. I understand that this is a singular evening and that something special is being prepared for dinner."

"Something special indeed," said the legislator.

"What do you have in store for us then?"

"That, gentlemen, is a surprise."

***

I woke with a start, surprised that I had been able to sleep. I thought I heard something, but I wasn't sure what it could be, nor if I had heard anything at all, or if my mind was creating illusions. I remained silent and listened, though I was distracted by a throbbing pain in my stomach, and I realized that I was famished and desperately thirsty.

I didn't know how long I had been a prisoner in this chamber, but it was long enough to drain my energy and leave me exasperated. I was exhausted and downtrodden, trying to avoid thoughts of what my fate would be, of how the distressing situation I was in might end.

Then I heard it again. This time, without a doubt, I had heard something: a distant sound that seemed like a creaking door opening. I stayed alert, scarcely able to contain my frenzy. I thought of my salvation, of being liberated from this prison, of seeing the light again, and I waited, waited for someone to come and open the door and allow me to escape.

So possessed was I by the hope of being freed, of walking the streets again, and so blinded as to contemplate the possibility that whoever was making the noises I had just heard could be the same person that plunged me into this hell, or an accomplice, or someone worse.

Then the sounds multiplied, equally muddled and distant. But there was no longer any doubt that something was going on outside. I sharpened my senses, completely focusing my attention: I heard vague murmurs and noises, like the sound of distant conversations happening on the other side of the walls. I tried to make sense of the things I was hearing and to figure out what could be causing them, so that I might form an idea of the place I was in; the sounds were distant and indiscernible. They could be almost anything, so the doubt and anxiety swelled up in me again. I was overwhelmed with hopelessness, and I felt once again the icy panic under my skin.

I waited. I kept waiting and listening. Now the uproar grew and the voices were closer, as if a group of people were carrying out some activity that at times brought them nearer to where I was confined. Then, I suddenly heard a metallic click that was crisp and clear, like the sound of a turning latch as a door opens. My heart skipped a beat in my chest. I heard footsteps and a voice of someone who seemed to be talking to themselves. Then I listened to the silence and the beating of my heart. I noticed that I was sweating and shaking. I kept waiting and listening. I was suddenly startled by the noise of something hitting the ground, followed by an exclamation which, for some reason, brought me hope. Undoubtedly someone was very close. This was my chance to make myself heard and give away my presence. I tried to speak, but it was impossible. I attempted to bang on the wall but couldn't. I kicked about fruitlessly and tried to no avail to keep from going crazy.

Then, with the most perfect clarity, I heard the words that I tried to make sense of; I tried to understand what key they might hold to elucidating the mystery of my captivity. The voice said clearly: two onions and three apples. Apples and onions. Did I hear correctly? I hesitated for a moment because I couldn't make sense of the words. But I couldn't mistrust my ears; I had absolutely heard clearly: onions and apples.

* * *

"Well sir, what do you say? You must be happy with your new little stretch of land," said the governor, addressing the tycoon. He smiled as he sent the governor a courteous and appreciative look.

"Good sir, you must know that you are among my most esteemed friends."

"What do you mean 'among them'? And I thought I would be your closest friend by now," said the governor with feigned surprise, the tone of his voice rising.

"Well, I'll hold you in that regard when you lend me your invaluable assistance in obtaining that nice little piece of land near the national park."

"But that tract of land is enormous! It's planned into the extension of the national park.

It is the only place in the province where a great number of endemic species reproduce, and it's the source of the drinking water for the neighboring towns. No sir, it's not possible."

"Of course it's possible!" replied the tycoon. "What's out of the realm of possibility is you turning your back on me. I thought we were friends. What's more, my proposal will be of great benefit to the surrounding villages, for they too need the soy, and the water will be better used to irrigate the farmland. Remember that mineral water is the healthiest and the best quality. Once it's bottled, the residents will be able to buy it without any problem at any one of my supermarkets. Believe me. I'm telling you, this is good for everyone.

"Believe me when I tell you that you're an extremely persuasive man," the governor said as he stood up, cigar in hand, and walked towards the large gold-framed mirror that adorned one of the walls of the room. In it danced the dazzling lights of a huge chandelier that hung from the ceiling. The governor looked at his own reflection. Clearly visible on his face was the satisfaction and pride with which he regarded himself, and the joy of being who he was, a man so lofty, so masterful, so powerful.

There was a glint in his eyes, and a thought grew in his mind, a brilliant idea.

"There might be a way," he said finally, as a smile spread across his face.

"But of course there's a way!" exclaimed the tycoon eagerly as he sprang to his feet. "I never doubted that our friendship would continue to strengthen. Just tell me: what is it that you want, what can I offer you, what can I do for you?"

At that moment, the gigantic clock on the wall struck one more hour with its successive chimes, and one of the servants entered the room to serve the gentlemen their vermouth as a sweet aroma of fresh herbs penetrated the room, saturating the air.

"It seems that dinner is almost ready," said the legislator.

"Yes, sir," replied the servant, "dinner will be served shortly."

"But when are you going to tell us about this zealously guarded dinner surprise that you have in store for us?" asked the industrialist.

"Is it rhino meat? There are very few of them left in the world now. If we don't try it soon, we may miss the opportunity forever."

"Dear friends, what I have prepared for you is the most unexpected of dishes, and I would dare to assert that you have never tasted such a meat."

***

The murmur I had heard at first was now a roar. Clearly the number of people outside where I was confined had multiplied, and their activity seemed more urgent or hectic.

My condition had worsened significantly, and it was now impossible for me to restrain the apprehension that consumed me, like a black ocean in which I slowly foundered. The torment of hunger and thirst was unbearable; every cell of my body tortured me with the need for sustenance, and the uncertainty of not knowing what dark design kept me in this place under these subhuman conditions, was wreaking havoc upon my sanity. Overwhelmed by the desperate situation in which I found myself, I was trying to calm down and organize my thoughts, when the metallic click of a door sounded once more.

A vain hope flooded my heart. Once again, the possibility, or the fantasy of escape burst in my consciousness, along with the hope of seeing the sun again and breaking free of this confinement. I heard voices and footsteps nearby and the sound of one object tipping against another. Again, I tried to thrash about and yell. I got as close as I could to the spot where the voices were coming from and tried to bang against it, scratch at it, to do something, anything that might arouse the attention of the people I had just heard. It was all in vain. I couldn't make my presence known. I couldn't let them know that I was in this place, suffering and going mad. Once again, it was only with the uttermost effort that I was able to control myself. I focused my attention on the voices I was hearing. They were having a conversation.

"So are the gentlemen vegetarian?"

"Vegetarian? Of course not, why, meat is almost the only thing they eat. The chef said something special was to be prepared for them."

"But there's no lamb, duck, or pork in this kitchen; the butcher came yesterday, and he only left some portions of liver for the pâté."

"Could you grab me the tomatoes please? I don't know what's being prepared for them tonight, but it's something special, and it's meat, believe me. They always eat meat, and they eat it raw too; they like the taste of blood."

"Of blood?" asked one of the voices as they walked away.

Then I heard the sound of the door closing once again. Now I knew that I was in a kitchen, and this knowledge only exasperated me further. For what unfathomable reason could I be gagged and hidden in this hellish hole as the prisoner of a chef? In my head the fantasies danced like ghosts in a dream. A grim notion of my fate replaced a horrendous fear; an icy panic spread over me like morning frost, and I fell into utter terror. Then I lost consciousness and faded into a lethargy that was both restful and comforting, a brief respite to forget the horrible misery I was in.

But it didn't last long. Once more, the click of the door brought me back to consciousness. Again, I heard footsteps approaching the place where I was confined. There was a pause. Very close to me, I heard the sound of a heavy piece of furniture being dragged along the floor. Then, with a start, I heard a key enter a lock that was close, very close, right next to me. I was paralyzed with anticipation, but then nothing happened, and the moment seemed eternal. Then I heard a crack, and a faint light illuminated my prison as a door started to open. My eyes opened immeasurably wide, but the sudden brightness hurt them. For a moment I was blinded. When I regained my vision, I found a man in front of me. My eyes automatically fell on the words embroidered on his jacket: "Chef de Cuisine." In his right hand he wielded a long, sharp kitchen knife, like a saber.

***

"I imagine that you too must be happy and satisfied at this moment," said the legislator addressing the industrialist.

"Of course I am. Believe me, I couldn't be a happier man right now, seeing as how business is moving forward as prosperously I could hope for."

"So those little problems you had with your slaves have been resolved?"

"Please, sir, don't use that word!" exclaimed the industrialist, but a smile crept across his face, and a sparkle ignited in his eyes. "They don't belong to me. I merely obtain the maximum benefit from their work and effort for the minimum possible salary. There's nothing wrong with that. It is perfectly honest, natural, and ethical; moreover, and above all, it is completely legal."

"Legal without a doubt it is, and it could not be otherwise for the duration of our friendship," the legislator replied as he leaned back in his comfortable, ample velvet armchair, which resembled a royal throne, and he took a long puff of his cigar.

For a moment his gaze was distracted by the smoke that ascended in spirals and was lost among the images of the fresco that adorned the ceiling.

"If there is anything I can do for you, anything you need, dear friend, you need only say the word; you know that we are here to help each other," the legislator said finally.

"Being that you are so generously disposed, my esteemed friend, I wonder what the possibilities are of legally annulling certain rights of my subjects that are causing me some inconvenience."

"Are you referring to their vacation and health benefits?"

"I'm referring to all of their undesirable rights!" said the industrialist with a fierce expression and a fleeting fire in his eyes.

The remaining members of the gathering exchanged complicit glances, mocking smiles stretching across their faces.

"But then you really do believe in slavery," said the governor.

"I believe in survival of the fittest. I believe that the strong must prevail and the weak must perish. I believe in our superiority as powerful men. I believe that a sublime and supreme blood runs in our veins. I believe, above all, in our friendship, in the things that we can achieve together.

The attendees of the meeting once again exchanged complicit and satisfied glances.

"Yes, sir," said the governor, "you speak the truth, and naturally we share your ideas about the social order. You are quite right; our friendship can manifest even the most audacious of dreams."

The massive ebony door opened once more to make way for the servant.

"Gentlemen," he announced, "dinner is served."

***

Sweet child, sweet visions bring your dreams. These are the things that you have to know, in order for you understand your duty and your extraordinary purpose, the role that is yours to fulfill, and the class of men among whom you must take your rightful place: men of supremacy, of shining metal, men of power, who control the future of lesser men, those who know the sweet taste of human flesh, to whom this world belongs and whose duty it is to direct and control it; it is their ranks you must join, and you will follow your path alongside them.

Now, sweet dear child, you know your duty and the role you have to fulfill. Now, beautiful child, child of power, now you know who you are.

***

The boy rolled over in his bed, shuddered, and then turned around. From between his warm little lips an exclamation escaped. His mother heard this timid sound and went over to the bed where her tender lamb, her sweet angel, was resting, and she saw him wake up and his little eyes slowly open.

"Hello, my love," she said to him tenderly. "How is my beautiful boy?"

"Mom, I had a dream," he replied in a voice soft and timid, like the whisper of a flower.

"A dream, my love? And do you remember what it was about?"

"Yes, Mom, I remember. It was a message for me."

"And what was the message?"

"I know what I want to be when I grow up now."

Honolulu, November 2018

THE FINAL TALE

MY dear, gullible reader, I want you to know that you have fallen into a trap. I want you to know that it is too late, that you are already doomed. One way or another, the book fell into your hands, you opened it, you turned its pages, you read them. Subtly, imperceptibly, a spiritual poison, a curse, has been working on you, and you welcomed it and accepted it. Now it is inexorably yours.

The book you are about to finish reading is in fact a cursed book, an evil book, whose only purpose is to spread its venom and poison the soul of the unwary reader who, like you, commit the reckless folly of reading it. This poison is implacable and deadly, it is also inescapable. This means that you are doomed, your soul has been irreversibly contaminated.

You did not notice it, nor did you suspect it, but that does not in the least alter the fact that the act was committed and that your soul, in a gradual fashion, or violently and suddenly, shall be plunged into a bottomless abyss of suffering, into a very inferno. Every one of the stories in this book conceals a damaging seed that is absorbed by the unsuspecting reader and grows within them, branches and multiplies, and ultimately invades them completely and leads them to their doom.

This is the purpose of each of its tales, which they carry out in ineluctable fashion, some directly, others more obliquely. Those dealing with warm or spiritual themes are the most harmful, the most noxious. If you read this book through, from the first story to this last, then naïve reader, by this point in the book, your soul has been completely steeped in its wicked poison, and it is your fate to burn in the flames of the abyss, the netherworld, the chasm of pain.

Your misfortune may, however, not be immediate. Your transformation and your corruption may be gradual, and if so far you have felt no damaging deviation in your character, this is because the book is working its slow poison on you. In any event, you can rest perfectly assured that this transformation will take place and that you will become a malignant person, a worker of evil, and will spread this corruption to the world around you before the book and its toxin ruins you and plunges you into its pit of woe, of infinite misery.

Yet I shall offer you one vain hope, a false way out, because I know that, right at this moment, you will be willing to clutch at anything to avoid descending into the maw gaping at your feet.

You may find it useful to know that there is a belief—necessarily false—that it is possible to escape the curse now maturing within you like some implacable virus.

A circle of enlightened persons have, over the centuries, developed a plan of action, which, if meticulously followed, may act as an antidote to the poison infecting you. This plan of action consists of a series of patters of behavior which they called "The Basic Principles".

In the thirteenth century, one member of this group of sages was rash enough to call these principles as "The New Commandments". Such temerity turned out wretchedly for him, for the Church considered it blasphemy and condemned this reckless man to be burned at the stake in order to cleanse his soul and make amends to the Holy Faith for this slur. But Cardinal Natolius was of the opinion that, in order to supply this vile sinner with true spiritual cleansing, he must be subjected to purification through supreme pain, and he therefore became a resident of the torture chambers before being delivered to the flames of the pyre. The Council felt that such a measure would be of great use to the spiritual development of the accused and would also discourage other foolish men from offering such affronts to God's Holy Church.

This circle of enlightened men that developed the Basic Principles contended that their constant daily practice could ease or completely eradicate the burden of the curse which the book released in its readers, provided these Principles were practiced with a sincere intention of the soul and at every possible opportunity.

The Church, in its constant war against the profane, ruled that a circle capable of producing anyone as irreverent as this man, burned at God's stake for his insult, was in turn responsible for such irreverence, and it therefore set about persecuting and punishing each of the members of the circle whenever it came upon them, and took systematic care in destroying all extant copies of the Basic Principles. Some, though, were concealed and protected, and have survived.

The Basic Principles, as originally stated, are as follows:

1. *Always show respect for one's own self, for the birds of the sky, for the grass that grows on the earth, for the insects and for every creature great and small.*

2. *Always act in a way that expresses the ideals of peace, understanding, concord, harmony and insight.*

3. *Feel love for everything existing and express it consistently.*

4. *Help to bring closer and to unite the peoples of the earth.*
5. *Practice compassion and always act in a way that eases one's own and others' suffering.*
6. *Express the truth in all our words and actions.*
7. *Show solidarity and contribute to one's own and others' wellbeing with every act.*
8. *Forgive any offenses and answer them with acts of kindness.*
9. *Contribute to the growth and development of all the creatures of creation in every way you can.*
10. *Be generous at every turn.*

As I said, there is a belief that, through observation and constant practice of these guidelines, one may escape the sentence imposed by reading the book, that or leaven its consequences. Yet this has never been demonstrated, there is no concrete evidence for it, and I know that it is not true.

Honolulu, December 2018

Table of contents

Made in the USA
Monee, IL
03 April 2024